THE GIRL RETREATS

THE GIRL RETREATS

THE LAST VAMPIRE™ BOOK 7

JUDITH BERENS   MARTHA CARR   MICHAEL ANDERLE

DISRUPTIVE IMAGINATION

Copyright © 2019 Judith Berens, Martha Carr and Michael Anderle
Cover by Fantasy Book Design
Cover copyright © LMBPN Publishing
A Michael Anderle Production

LMBPN Publishing
PMB 196, 2540 South Maryland Pkwy
Las Vegas, NV 89109

First US edition, October 2019
Version 1.01, October 2019
eBook ISBN: 978-1-64202-508-8
Print ISBN: 978-1-64202-509-5

DEDICATIONS

From Martha

To everyone who still believes in magic
and all the possibilities that holds.
To all the readers who make this
entire ride so much fun.
And to my son, Louie and so many wonderful friends who
remind me all the time of what
really matters and how wonderful
life can be in any given moment.

From Michael

To Family, Friends and
Those Who Love
To Read.
May We All Enjoy Grace
To Live The Life We Are
Called.

CHAPTER ONE

W hat a long day. Craig pulled the lever on the side of his recliner to extend it and take the pressure off his feet. *All that yard work, running around to pick up the girls... I know I'm not exactly looking forward to them learning to drive this summer, but man, I could use a break.*

He retrieved the remote from the side table near his chair and turned the TV on. Both girls were in their bedrooms, so he was free to watch whatever he wanted. He selected the *GUIDE* button on his remote and scrolled through the channels.

On one of the stations, a nightly news magazine-style program was on. It was called *The Evening Buzz*, a cheesy name that always evoked an eye-roll from him whenever he saw it.

When he scrolled past it, he glanced at the description of that evening's episode. He expected it to be something useless and overly sensational, like a drugged-out mother who murdered her family or some kind of fake epidemic story designed to instill fear in the minds of the audience.

The description that evening, however, did catch his attention.

Did a superhero save a little dog? We look at the video evidence and talk with a bystander who witnessed it with his own eyes.

With a long and dramatic sigh, he clicked the button on the remote to turn the show on. *This story won't go away on its own, will it?*

"Hey, girls! Get in here." He paused the live feed until they arrived in the living room.

"What's up, Dad? I was in the middle of something."

"Yeah, I was talking to Eric."

He pointed to the couch. "Have a seat. We all need to see how bad this is."

Alexis and Vickie exchanged confused glances before they walked over to the couch and sat as he pressed the *PLAY* button. The deep voice of an overdramatic narrator spoke over the security feed recording from the traffic camera.

The footage was black-and-white and grainy enough that there could be some doubt as to the accuracy of it. The narrator, however, clearly believed what he was seeing.

It moved slowly, frame by frame, to let the viewers examine it for themselves. In one, the small dog stood innocently in the middle of the intersection and the car that barreled toward it was only a few feet away from annihilating the poor thing.

But in the very next frame, a figure darted in—she appeared to materialize out of thin air—and pounded into the front of the car. The impact was immediate, and the vehicle was damaged significantly but also knocked off-course and away from the dog.

The narrator spoke breathlessly throughout each frame of the footage.

"Is it real, or is it a carefully-crafted hoax? Millions of people have watched and re-watched this footage from a security camera in Milwaukee, WI. In it, a figure appears from nowhere to destroy a car and save the life of a small dog. But, as more and more people discover the video, the debate rages on. Was this the act of a superhero or is all this simply made up? One man claims to know the answer."

On that last sentence, the footage switched to an African American man in khakis and a dark green polo shirt seated in a chair across from one of the show's many interviewers.

"I saw it with my own eyes. It was a teenage girl, and she came in so fast you couldn't blink or you'd miss her completely. She ran directly into the car."

They showed more footage of the interview as the narrator continued.

"This is Dylan Jones. He says he was on the sidewalk at that intersection when it all happened. And regardless of whether or not this was the act of a superhero, a monster, or some otherworldly creature, he claims it absolutely happened—and he has the video to prove it."

Craig glanced at Vickie and shook his head. "I sure wish this story would go away."

She met his gaze, her expression chagrined. "Tell me about it. It's hard enough trying to be normal around here."

"Did you really have to do this, though?" The tone of Alexis' voice hinted at exasperation. "This looks really bad."

Her tone immediately put the vampire on the defensive. "What was I supposed to do? Let the poor puppy get flattened? How was I supposed to know that someone would be there with a camera?"

The TV show switched to the color footage of Vickie recorded by the witness. Her face was mostly covered, and she ran away quickly enough that it was difficult to recognize her—unless you knew her personally.

The camera work did nothing to improve the video, either. As Dylan pursued her down the sidewalk, the recording shook and trembled, which made the view blurry and even more difficult to see clearly.

Over and over again, the footage switched from that on Dylan's phone—slowed to a crawl in an effort to reveal who she was—and more frame-by-frame shots of her colliding with the car from the traffic camera.

Meanwhile, the interview continued.

"I know what I saw. Maybe people won't believe their eyes or they'll think that this is doctored footage somehow but look at it. You see the side mirror break off and hang by a wire, which is how the car was found. You see the airbag deploy. It had gone off by the time the paramedics and the police arrived. Everything in this video matches perfectly with what the authorities found when they reached the scene. I'm not saying I can explain it. I didn't believe my eyes either. But I also know that I saw it. A teenage girl materialized and crashed into the car. It didn't hit a pole, or another car, or whatever. It hit this girl. She came out without a scratch on her, and the car was severely damaged. And when I chased her, she disappeared."

As he spoke that last sentence, the show displayed the end of his video, where he turned the corner and Vickie was gone—having tapped into her super-speed.

The segment took up about half the program and repeatedly showed the impact with the car and her sprinting away from the scene. Finally, *The Evening Buzz* changed topics to the story of a husband and his mistress working together to convince his wife that she was going insane to end the marriage without having to worry about settlements. It was more typical *Buzz* fare, and Craig couldn't wait to turn it off.

"I feel like I have to take a shower every time I watch that show." He shuddered. "Okay, we still need to talk about this."

"What's there to talk about?" Vickie asked and frowned at him. "I was caught on camera, but no one seems to agree on whether or not it's legitimate. I think I got out of this one." She gave Alexis a hopeful glance.

The other girl sided with her father, however. "I…don't think so. You barely got out of this. Every time you use your powers, it seems like you come closer and closer to being caught. And I don't know what will happen if someone does finally catch you."

"She's right." Craig lowered the footrest on his chair and leaned forward. "If you are caught, you could be in serious trouble. Someone could get their hands on you somehow and you would have no choice but to go with them. Who knows what they would do to you? And we wouldn't be able to do anything about it."

5

The vampire exhaled angrily. "My instinct is to help. Why would anyone try to stop that?"

"You may see yourself as a hero, but every time you save something, you hurt something else. For every action, there is an equal but opposite reaction." He folded his hands and rested them on his stomach. "I think we need to put a moratorium on using your powers."

"I don't know what that means." She scowled.

"It means no more powers," Alexis explained. "And I'm kinda with him on this. You can't keep using your powers openly like that. Like…you know what he's saying about an equal but opposite reaction? You saved that dog, but you also destroyed another man's car and put him in the hospital."

Vickie raised her palms. "Okay, but he'll survive. If he had run the dog over—"

"We understand the why, Vickie." He struggled to explain to her that they knew what her brain was thinking, but regardless, she still caused problems. "Intention isn't the issue here. We know you're a good-hearted person who tries to do good in the world. But you're still a teenager, and while you might have control over your powers, you need to exercise better judgment on when to use them."

She stood from the couch, ready to storm away from the conversation. "You bring a vampire here and then tell her not to be a vampire. I don't get it."

Her sister rose to face her. "That's not it, Vickie. We're trying to protect you. This video on TV and online could still come back to bite you. Someone out there could make the connection and you would be stuck. The only way to prevent others from finding out about you is to not give them the chance."

Vickie stared at the beige carpet of the living room while she mulled over whether or not they were right. *They mean well. They're coming from the right mindset. You can sense that. But can you stop being a vampire entirely?*

"What happens if someone is in trouble? I can save so many people—and already have. Am I supposed to ignore them? Let them be killed or maimed or whatever else might happen?"

Craig tilted his head sympathetically. "Yeah. Bad things happen all the time in this world. You can't stop all of them. And if you get caught, not only will those continue, but similar things will almost certainly happen to you as well. No one wants that. You'll have to fight your instincts. I think it's the only way out of this."

Without another word, the vampire retreated to her bedroom and laid on her bed. For a moment, she relived the experience of saving that dog.

There was something immensely satisfying to her about what she had done. But it wasn't only the act of goodwill. She had loved colliding with the steel of the car and shattering the headlight while the metal wrapped around her shoulder as she struck it with all her might. The impact was more than simply satisfying. She couldn't put her finger on why, but it was.

Although she moved at lightning speed, the moment of impact felt like it happened in slow motion. She saw the shards of glass spew up from the windshield. The slow crunch and grind of metal as it buckled beneath her went on forever, it seemed.

But when she thought about it, her mind did drift to the other two people in the area—the driver and the witness.

She felt bad that the driver was hurt, even though she knew he would be fine. And the witness was the entire reason for this mess, although he couldn't really be blamed for being in that particular place at that particular time.

There's no way for me to sense whether or not a witness is there. At least, not in a reasonable amount of time. They may be right. If I want to survive in this world, I think I have to stop being a vampire.

The prospect broke her heart but she knew it was the right thing to do. Now, though, the question wasn't whether or not she should do it but something far more intense.

Can I even do this? Am I able to control my instincts and fight any instinct to save anyone or fight anyone? Having my powers has been one of the joys of this new life and using them regularly feels so good. Can I ignore all that and simply be normal?

CHAPTER TWO

E ric was still bleary-eyed when he walked into the
bathroom during his lunch hour. He'd struggled for
the entire morning to make it through his classes and felt
no better than he had when he'd first dragged himself out
of bed.

After using the bathroom, he paused at the sink and
stared into the mirror while he washed his hands. *You look
terrible, man.* His eyes were bloodshot and dark circles
shadowed his face under his eyes, and his pale skin made
them seem even worse. *You look like you have been in a
hospital bed for a week.*

While he hadn't been sick, he hadn't slept well at all.
After he saw the viral video of Vickie crushing the car, he
knew he had to ask her about it. Even though a part of him
needed to know the truth, he was also terrified of the
answer.

All weekend long, his mind had strained to make sense
of the situation. *If it's her and the video is legit, what does that
mean for us? I can't date someone with super-powers, can I?*

Would our kids have super-powers? Does that mean she's not a girl at all? What does any of this even mean?

Over and over, he repeated those questions and other similar ones until he finally collapsed from exhaustion. Invariably, he'd wake up an hour later and repeat the cycle again.

Now, as he stood in front of the bathroom mirror under the already-unflattering fluorescent lightbulbs over his head, he realized he had taken it too far. *You have to ask someone. You have to talk about this. If you bottle this up inside, you'll be dead by the end of the week.*

He dried his hands under the blow-dryer, retrieved the brown paper bag with his lunch that he'd set on the bathroom counter, and walked out to the cafeteria.

Once he sat and opened the bag, Alexis greeted him with a smile. "Hey."

"Hey."

"What's wrong with you? You look like garbage."

Eric pulled a meatloaf sandwich from the bag. "Gee, thanks."

She laughed. "You know I didn't mean it like that. What's the problem? Are you sick?"

A yawn prevented an immediate answer and he removed the top slice of bread from the sandwich and tore a ketchup packet open. "Nah, I didn't sleep well last night." He squirted the condiment onto the meatloaf and replaced the top slice of bread again.

Alexis glanced at his sandwich and sneered. "Nothing a cold loaf of meat can't fix. What is with the cold meatloaf sandwich? That looks disgusting."

Gleefully, he took an enormous bite and chewed. "It's

actually delicious. My whole family is really into these. It's almost better than eating regular meatloaf hot. We live for cold meatloaf sandwiches."

She twisted her face and curled her lip. "No thanks."

He shrugged. "More for me."

The girl picked up the slice of pizza in front of her and raised it to her mouth to tear a bite off with her teeth. "But other than your terrible taste in food, what's your problem? Are you not sleeping because something's bugging you, or is something bad at home?"

Eric raised an eyebrow. "What's with all the questions?"

"I've known you for long enough that I can tell when something is bothering you. Spill." Her gaze challenged him over her bottle of milk.

For a moment, he considered changing the subject. *She knows Vickie better than anyone. If I ask her, I could still ruin everything. I don't want that. I should simply move on and ignore it.*

But the more he tried to protest, the deeper she dug her heels in. She knew something was bothering her friend, and she decided she'd continue to pry until she felt she had an honest answer from him.

"Is it Vickie?" Alexis leaned in. "Is something wrong with you two?" He paused and tried to think of a good response but she read his hesitation as confirmation. "Oh, no. It is, isn't it? Did you two break up? Do you want to break up with her? I was afraid this would happen."

He waved his hand quickly to stop her. "No, no. It's not that. Things are great between us. I only...can I ask you a question about her?"

"Sure."

"Is there something...I don't know, different about her?"

The question caught her off-guard and she swallowed awkwardly. "No. What do you mean?"

Eric put his sandwich down. "I don't know. Like, does she...is she..." He couldn't quite decide how to end that sentence. Finally, he closed his eyes and mustered up the confidence to open up to his old friend. "Have you seen that video going around of the girl who pounds into the car and crushes it?"

Her stomach knotted immediately but she did her best to avoid showing it on her face. "Yeah, I've seen it. Who hasn't?"

He looked at the can of soda next to his sandwich. A lone drop of condensation moseyed its way slowly down the side and onto the table. "Well, I think...this is going to sound stupid...but I think that's Vickie in the video."

She tried to mask her panic. "Really? Come on, that can't be possible." *Boy, housing a vampire sure makes you lie a lot to keep the operation under control.*

"I don't know what's possible and what isn't." He shrugged uncomfortably. "I've tried my best to make sense of it. But it's clearly someone from our high school or someone who owns a Clear Lake cross country shirt for some reason. I think it looks like her, and I wouldn't be surprised if it was her."

Alexis' brain definitely moved into panic. *What do I say? I can't tell him that he's right. I can't say, "Well, gee, she's a vampire, dude." Do I have to sit here and take this? Or do I have to lie about it forever so I can cover for her? Shoot.*

"I know, it's crazy." He picked his sandwich up again.

"But I definitely think it looks like her. Maybe it's not. But I don't know. Do you know anything about it?"

I know everything about it. "No, I really don't. I'm not sure there's anything to know. I think the video is fake, personally. Either someone is out there using deep-fakes and making it look like Vickie is the one in the video, or it's simply a coincidence."

"Not me." Eric shoved the last of his meatloaf sandwich into his mouth. "I can tell that it's real. It's the real deal, man. It definitely happened. There's an eyewitness, and both videos are independently verified. It has to be real. In my book, there's no way this is a fake."

"Then what are we looking at?" *This is a good opportunity to get outside perspective, I suppose. I can try to think of this as a good thing. He won't truly believe it's her anyway.* "What's your explanation for it?"

He paused for a moment and chewed silently before he swallowed. "It's obviously some kind of superpower. The dude who filmed it said the girl came out of nowhere, so she moves really fast. And she wasn't hurt by the impact. She's like The Flash or something."

The comparison amused Alexis, who had always mentally compared Vickie to other monsters since she was a vampire. *I've never really thought of her as a superhero, but I guess she is one.* "And you think Vickie is The Flash?" She tapped into any acting skill she had so her skepticism could sound convincing enough.

"I know it sounds a little crazy—"

"A little?" That was the perfect opportunity for her to lay it on thick. "Eric, you're talking about a girl I live with and you've dated for months. I feel like we would know something like that long before this video came out. Why are you even sweating it this much? It's probably not even her."

"It looks exactly like her."

"So what? With technology these days, they can put anyone anywhere. Deep-fakes are a thing, man." She felt confident she could sway his opinion if he could entertain the possibility that the videos were faked.

On a roll now, she pulled her phone out—which was allowed only during the lunch hour—and opened the YouTube app. "I saw one the other day that is so realistic it's creepy. Some guy took clips of *The Shining* and put Jim Carrey in it over the main guy, Jack whatever-his-name-is."

"Nicholson." Eric scowled in disappointment. "How can you forget that?"

"Anyway…" Alexis rolled her eyes while she swiped through the search results. "I don't know how they do it, but they paste his face on the head and blend it all together. It looks like Jim Carrey is in this movie. Here it is—see for yourself."

She passed him her phone and he watched a two-minute clip of what appeared to be Jim Carrey swinging an ax at a hotel room door while Shelley Duvall screamed on the other side. He smirked as he watched the video, which was really well done. By the time the fake Jim Carrey stuck his head through the door and shouted, "Heeeeere's John-ny," he was laughing.

Once it had finished, he set the phone down on the table. "That's hilarious. Who spends their time doing something like that?"

That was all the window she needed. "Exactly. These

people do it simply because they can. They like to see how many people they can fool, especially if they can get on the news. Some—like whoever created this clip— do it because they think it's fun. But if they can get news coverage of a video they put together, it feeds their ego. They enjoy watching the world freak out, that's all."

Eric crumpled the empty plastic sandwich baggie that once held his now-devoured meatloaf sandwich and rubbed the back of his neck. "I guess you could be right."

Okay, time to go for the jugular. "You love Vickie, right?"

"Yeah."

"And that means you trust her, right?"

"Yeah."

"Don't you think, if Vickie really did have super-powers or whatever, that she would tell you? It seems like something she would have shared by now. I know for a fact that Vickie loves you. She's crazy about you and would tell you if something about her was weird like that."

Instantly, she regretted saying that. *If he ever does find out, he'll be really mad at Vickie for lying to him, I bet. I've rated her love by whether or not she tells him that she's a vampire. That could come back to bite me. But right now, I have to get out of this conversation.*

The rest of the lunch hour was uneventful. They both finished eating while the conversation bounced between various subjects. When they separated to go to their classes, she felt confident that she had thrown him off the scent.

But as Eric walked down the hallway, his brain took over—and it had a whole new set of questions. *If it's a deepfake video, why wouldn't they show her face? Why fake a video like that if you won't actually reveal who did it? What's the point? And if it's a fake video, how did they get the police to think that it was from a traffic camera? Doesn't that feed go directly to the police? This makes zero sense if you really think about it.*

And his problem was that he did think about it. Every chance he could, his mind went back to that video, and every time, it came up with more questions than answers. Alexis hadn't helped him at all, and he began to wonder if she was hiding any of this, too.

CHAPTER THREE

A few miles down the road from the school, Jim Trembo strolled into Mayfair Mall across the busy street from his hotel.

He always hated going to the mall and he scowled the second he stepped through the automatic doors. Soft, inoffensive pop music blared over the sound system and drifted through the two levels of fashionable stores selling overpriced goods.

Even though the mall at midday on a Monday was much less offensive than the mall in the evening or on a weekend when the school-aged kids would take it over, there were still too many people there for his liking.

Jim dodged and scooted around various people who spent their day wandering in and out of the stores—the elderly mall walkers, mothers who pushed strollers with screaming toddlers and babies, and bleary-eyed third-shift workers who enjoyed their only opportunity to be among the living for a few hours before they had to head to their jobs.

He kept his focus directly ahead like he was a racing horse with blinders strapped to his face. *Get to the food court and ignore everything else.*

As always, there was varied competition for his attention. A middle-aged African American woman stood outside a tea shop, held a tray of little plastic shot glasses full of the Sample Of The Day, and beckoned passersby to stop for a taste. Several Asian men lurked in the middle of the mall with compact massage tables next to them, asking anyone and everyone if they wanted to relax for a moment and have the knots rubbed out of their shoulders. Even the toymakers tried to catch his eye and flew cheap plastic drones over his head to see if they could make an extra sale or two.

It's like these people don't know what to do with themselves. Why would I come to the mall and be convinced that I need any of those things? It was a familiar refrain that he repeated often in his mind whenever he was forced to walk through a shopping center with aggressive salespeople.

Finally, he managed to push free of the main level and onto an escalator, which took him past the Victoria's Secret display on his way to the food court. He shook his head. *I like how they make the display as big as physically possible so there's no chance you can avoid looking like a weirdo as you stare at women's underwear.*

He stepped off and glanced at the vaulted ceilings peppered with skylights. The high-noon sunshine beat down through the skylights over a section of tables and chairs in the middle of the mall. Several elderly couples were seated there to enjoy various food court fare and the brightness of the sunshine apparently didn't bother them at all.

Jim took a few steps away from the escalator and scanned the area. His gaze finally located Pete Stabone, who waved his hand over his head to catch his attention. He nodded at his colleague and moved quickly toward him.

When he approached the table, he noticed the man already sinking his teeth into a burger. "Couldn't wait for me, eh?"

Pete shrugged. "I was hungry. I didn't think you'd mind."

He looked up to study his options. "Nah, it's fine. Let me get something to eat quickly and we can chat."

Minutes later, he returned to the table with a tray holding a small soda and a carton filled with teriyaki chicken and white rice. He sat and opened it for the steam to escape so the food would cool.

The other man glanced at the meal. "No veggies?"

"They simply get in my way." He chuckled.

"Eh, you have to take better care of yourself." Pete pointed to the small side salad on his tray. "When you reach a certain age, you can't eat like you used to."

"Thanks, Mom. How's the burger?"

"It's okay. It's a food court burger." He put it down and opened his plastic salad carton. "So, to recap, we have this video of a girl trashing a car."

Jim nodded while he scooped chicken and rice with the little plastic fork that came with it. "Yes. I think this is the breakthrough we've been looking for. In my mind, there has to be a direct connection between this video and our own investigation."

JUDITH BERENS

Pete tore open a small packet of Italian dressing and squirted it onto the bed of lettuce, tomatoes, and shredded carrots. "Okay. And you still think it's real?"

"We've talked about this. It's from a traffic camera vetted by the police department. It has to be real."

"That's fine. How do we get closer to what we're looking for by using this video? I've seen it and you can't really see who it is. It's only a girl with dark hair."

His boss raised a finger. "No, it's not only a girl with dark hair." He pulled his phone out. "I took a few screen-shots and zoomed in on them to double-check what we thought we noticed the first time we saw it. Here, take a look. That sweatshirt definitely says *Clear Lake High School Cross Country Team*. This is a high school girl. It even has this year printed on it." He set the phone down on the table between them. "This girl is who we're looking for. She is the reason why we're digging in that field. Here is your supernatural activity, my friend."

"Okay."

"Okay?" Jim was indignant. "Okay? Pete, this is the smoking gun. This is the evidence we have searched for over the past few years. This video could lead us to everything we've ever wanted. It validates our careers. How can you not be more excited about this?"

Pete crunched a mouthful of salad and swallowed it. "Hey, I've been as excited as you throughout this project. But it's going too well. I'm waiting for the other shoe to drop, that's all."

"There are no other shoes. This is a high school girl recorded performing supernatural activity with both video evidence and an eyewitness. It doesn't get much more open-and-shut than that. Now, we simply have to find her."

"And how do you propose we do that? Go to the cops?"

He gritted his teeth and grimaced at the thought. "I really don't want to deal with local cops. You never know if they'll feel threatened by your presence or not. We're federal agents, remember. They have a tendency to resent you after a while, and I don't want anything to hinder our chances of obtaining the information we need. Besides, I don't want to deal with a middleman. It will merely waste time."

The answer confused the other man. "Then what are we supposed to do? Walk into the high school and ask?"

Jim lifted his soda to his lips. "Basically, yeah."

Pete uttered a hearty laugh. "That's your plan? Jeez, Jim, I had more faith in you than that."

"Okay, that's not exactly my plan. But that's why we're here. I'll need some kind of cover, right? Some story I can use to get access to the school and its students so I can have a closer look at whoever this person is."

"You don't think saying, 'Hey, I think one of your students is an alien or other supernatural being,' will give you the access you need?" He smirked at his own little joke.

His boss wasn't amused. "Do you want to help me or not?"

"Fine. How about a reporter? You work for the...uh, Journal or whatever the newspaper is here and are doing a feature on high school athletes."

There was a fairly long silence while he considered that and the possible ramifications. "I don't know. I feel like that would open too many other issues. For one, I don't think it will allow me much access. And two, what if someone has a dad or a mom or family member who already works for the paper? My cover could be blown immediately."

Pete thought about it, then nodded and took another mouthful of his salad. "Okay, so you have your government ID already. Tell 'em you're a federal agent. That way, you're not lying and there's nothing to check on."

"What is a federal agent doing in a high school in Milwaukee, though? I can't simply walk in there and demand that they let me in because I'm a federal agent."

The other man frowned and began to think out loud. "What would be interesting enough that the feds would get involved? What are issues facing high school athletes?"

They discussed their options and bounced various ideas off one another. Athletes and their dating lives. Teen drug use. Athletics and academics. Nothing seemed to quite fit what they were looking for.

Finally, Jim snapped his fingers. "I know—doping."

Pete shut the now-empty salad container. "Doping? Seriously? That's more of a problem with the pros."

"Anything can be a problem for a high school if we say it's a problem for the high school. Think about it, Pete. We'll say it's a new thing we want to investigate. It's a new public health crisis. Teens are having hormone therapy all the time. Maybe we suspect they are being given additional testosterone to enhance their strength and endurance. It could be a believable scenario—like the trickle-down effect from substance abuse in the pros."

The other man leaned back in his chair and folded his

arms in front of him. "Do you think kids are that competitive?"

"Absolutely. In certain parts of this country, kids are doing whatever they physically can simply to have an advantage in sports. I think it totally fits. Think of the parents of some of these athletes. They're either living out their fantasies through their kids, or they're trying to validate their own parenting by forcing their kids to be successful. They'll do anything to get their kids to first place. That's what makes this believable."

"I suppose we could frame it as some kind of public health crisis. But why pick Clear Lake High School?"

"That's the easy part. It's done at random. We're investigating all kinds of schools. Clear Lake happened to be next in line, that's all. Plus, I can use my ID badge and my real name, so we don't have to worry about getting anything else issued or having to remember my fake name, or whatever."

A pause followed while Pete sipped his water. "I think you've found it. This can work. And if you focus on athletes, you should be able to learn more about the distance runners there—you'll have access to the coaches too. It opens the right doors."

"And that's all we need, Pete." Jim scooped up another mouthful of his lunch confidently. "That's all we need. If we open the right doors, we can find this girl and bring her in as quickly as possible. Everything about this investigation has fallen into place. This is the next logical step."

"And you're not waiting for the other shoe to drop?" His colleague sighed. "I am merely anxious that everything will fall apart."

"It's meant to be this time, Pete. We have finally found what we've looked for and we will walk away as heroes. Everything about this is perfect. We'll actually get our hands on a supernatural being, and we'll put it to work for us. Our department will be the heroes of the federal government after this."

CHAPTER FOUR

Craig sighed deeply and irritably as he climbed out of his SUV. He slammed the door shut, stepped to his right, and opened the door to the back seat. With a scowl settled on his face, he pulled his laptop bag out and slung it over his shoulder before he closed the door once again.

I hate distractions and I hate interruptions. I have so much to do today before the girls get home from school. He looked at the old white sign with faded red lettering that hung over the building in front of him. *Wright Auto Repair.*

He shook his head and crossed the small parking lot. *This place is always so tiny and greasy. It's almost impossible to get any work done here. But what am I supposed to do? I'm probably lucky the SUV made it here, in the first place.*

The previous day, he had noticed the warning light for the battery blaze red on his dashboard. Everything still functioned normally, but he knew that wasn't a good sign. Back in high school, he drove an old Dodge Neon that had the same problem. When he parked the car in front of his then girlfriend's house, he couldn't get it started again because the battery was dead, which left him stranded.

He worried the same thing would happen and knew he shouldn't take the chance. Fortunately, Wright Auto Repair was down the road from his house. He was able to get the vehicle started without issues, though, and he willed it to continue to work until he arrived—with the radio, headlights, and anything else he could think of switched off.

Craig yanked the door open and it jingled a little bell hung overhead. Before he stepped inside, he took a deep breath of fresh air, knowing the sharp smell of axle grease and tire rubber would overwhelm his senses for the next couple of hours.

He wiped his feet on the mat and looked ahead to see a beautiful woman seated behind the counter. *That's not Bill. What happened to him?*

Bill was usually the guy who worked the front desk at the shop. He was older and stout with thick-framed glasses and a mustache that covered the opening to his mouth when he closed it. His balding head was always covered with a hat bearing the brand name of a set of tires or motor oil—whatever was free and lying around.

The man's replacement, however, was a pleasant surprise and ensured that he wouldn't be upset for very long. *She is cute. Much cuter than Bill.*

The woman smiled a perfect white smile at him as he approached. She tucked her auburn hair behind her ear and leaned forward to fold her hands on the desk in front of her. Her bright blue eyes almost made him forget where he was.

Still, he shook it off. "Hi, I have an appointment for this morning. It's under Watson."

She nodded to him and straightened to type on the computer. "Craig?"

"That's me."

"Great. I'll need the keys. Do you have it parked out front?"

He pointed over his shoulder with his thumb. "Yep. It's the only SUV out there." As he spoke, he couldn't help but stare into her eyes. He suddenly no longer minded the axle grease smell that had been so irksome only moments before.

She took the keys from him. "Do you plan to wait or do you need me to give you a call when it's ready?"

"I'll wait, actually." He lifted his laptop bag and patted it with a smile. "I have work to do." *Why are you being so cheesy right now? Be cool, man.*

She giggled. "Awesome. Well, you can have a seat over there and get comfortable. There's water in the corner if you get thirsty. My name's Amanda if you need anything, okay?"

"That sounds great, Amanda. Thank you." He smiled warmly at her and walked over to the row of chairs pressed up against the wall. He sat on one and hoped that the visible dirt and grime on the old purple fabric wouldn't rub off onto his pants.

Stretched in front of him was an old coffee table— clearly taken from someone's home after about thirty years —littered with *Sports Illustrated* and *Car and Driver* magazines that were at least six months old.

In the middle of the table was a small glass bowl with a

single Tootsie Roll in it. Resigned to his current predicament, Craig unzipped his laptop bag and withdrew his computer. He flipped it open and entered the Wi-Fi password that was posted on the wall opposite him.

"Oh!" Amanda spun on her chair and bent down to disappear from view. He looked up from his laptop screen and stared in her direction, curious as to what she would be looking for.

After a few seconds of rustling, she emerged with a large plastic bag filled with Tootsie Rolls and other candy. She rounded the corner of the desk and walked over with a silly smile on her face. "Sorry about that. Some days, we go through four bowls of this, and then a bowl will last three weeks. I can never predict it."

"Don't worry about it." He waved his hand confidently. "I won't eat them so fast."

"No, no. Eat all you want. I simply have to stay on top of it, that's all." She nodded at his laptop. "What do you do?"

Craig wore a sheepish grin. "I'm a podcaster." *Why are you still embarrassed to admit that?* The old news reporter in him felt like he was telling people that he played around on the Internet for a living or something. *You have an awesome career in new media. Be proud of yourself.*

Like many people, Amanda reacted with surprise—and looked impressed. "Really? That's so cool. I listen to a few of them myself. What is your podcast about?"

She already knows podcasts. You don't have to explain your career. That's a plus. "I dig into real-world stories about issues that affect us all. Right now, I'm in the middle of a season about blended families."

She dropped the plastic bag of candy at her feet. "Oh, are you in a blended family? Or do you come from one?"

"I'm the head of one, I guess." He chuckled nervously. "It's me and my daughter, and we adopted my niece from Austria last summer. So we're navigating this new life together and talking about it." *There's that smile again. She has such an enchanting smile.*

"I know so many people who are in situations like that. Good for you for making it a focus. I would think many people could relate."

He pointed to his laptop screen. "Yeah, this podcast does fairly well. I make a living with it, and that's important."

"Totally." She nodded enthusiastically. "Does your wife work? Or did you say you had a wife? Sorry, I missed that part."

"Um…yeah, my wife passed away from cancer last year, so it's only me and the girls." *And here comes the sympathetic head-tilt.*

On cue, Amanda tilted her head and pressed her lips together. "I'm so sorry to hear that."

Craig chuckled. "It's okay. Really. It's definitely not something I would recommend going through, but my daughter and I are doing great now and moving forward with our lives." *Change the subject. Don't only talk about your-self.* "How long have you worked here? I'm so used to seeing Bill behind the counter."

She laughed and turned her head to look at the counter where she had sat. "Yeah, Bill actually retired a couple of months ago. I mean, he retired." She made air quotes with her fingers. "He still comes in and works the desk a few days a week. I'm only here to kinda fill in when needed. I'm usually here two or three days a week, depending on how he feels."

Okay, she has a flexible job. That means she must be married to someone supporting her. Or dating someone anyway. "What does your husband do?"

She shook her head. "I'm not married anymore. My husband left me about six months ago."

What a fool. "I'm sorry, I didn't know."

"Oh, no, of course you didn't. Relax, it's fine. My son and I have had healing time in recent months. Besides, I learned quickly that no one wants to hang out with you if you constantly complain about your ex-husband. I started to learn how to deal with it on my own and come out the other end a little stronger than before."

At this point, Craig closed his laptop. *It's not like I'm getting any work done right now anyway.* "It sounds like you have the right attitude. How old is your son?"

"He's six so he's in school during the day, which is great. That makes life a little easier for me. And we get the child support check and everything—my ex is good about that. But I needed to get back into the workforce and get experience. Plus, it helps to have a little spending money."

He glanced around the room. "Do you like working here?"

She shrugged. "It's okay. It's not exactly a glamorous job, but for people who haven't really held anything down for a decade, glamor isn't something I can hold out for." Amanda laughed, which prompted him to smile again. "But everyone here is nice, and it seems like the guys doing the work out there are honest. I was worried about that. You never know with mechanics."

She has integrity, she has a positive attitude, and she's single.

"Anyway, I have a few follow-up calls to make. And I don't want to keep you from your work. I'll be over there if you need anything, okay?"

Please keep me from my work. "That sounds good. Thanks, Amanda."

The woman moved back to her place behind the desk, tucked the bag of candy away, and began to shuffle through papers as she prepared to make a few calls.

Craig tried to stop himself from staring at her, opened his laptop, and went through various show notes as he brainstormed new episodes. Every once in a while, he'd glance at her and sometimes, caught her looking at him.

About two hours later, she called to him. "Craig. Your SUV is all set."

Smiling, he shut his laptop, stuffed it back into the bag, and walked over to her. *Don't look too eager, man. Why can't you be cool?* "Was it the alternator?"

"It was." Amanda placed a printout of the bill in front of him. "The total is two hundred and forty-three dollars."

He nodded glumly and handed a credit card over. "I've dealt with alternators before. I really wish I could have done this one on my own and saved the money."

She swiped his card and pressed a few buttons on the reader. "Yeah, alternators are kinda annoying. They are really easy to replace—you only need to swap it out—but it's getting at them that's the problem."

She knows her cars. I kinda like that. "That's exactly it,

31

yeah. Engines are so packed, it's not worth my time to take half of it apart with the tools I have."

"Well, that's why we're here." She stapled the printout of the receipt to the itemized bill and handed it to him, along with his card. "It was nice spending a couple of hours with you, Craig. I hope to see you again soon."

"Not too soon, I hope."

She shook her head when she realized what she'd said. "Oh, yeah. I won't wish auto repairs on you!"

He laughed. "I know. It was nice meeting you too, Amanda. See you soon."

Craig walked out into the parking lot. The sun blazed overhead and he squinted after being stuck inside for the past couple of hours. He was halfway across the parking lot when he stopped in his tracks.

What are you doing? Don't walk away. Go back there and ask her. The worst she can say is no and you won't see her again for months if you don't have to.

With a decisive nod, he spun on his heel and returned to the door. She raised her eyebrows when she saw him walk in. "Did you forget something?"

"Yeah." He marched up to the desk with a confident air that he hadn't had in quite some time. "Are you free for dinner on Friday night?"

CHAPTER FIVE

"I know you're a vampire and everything, but I'm about to lay a serious beating on you." Alexis smiled devilishly.

"Excuse me?" Vickie stepped back and pretended to be shocked. "That's serious big talk coming from someone who can only run...what, ten minutes a mile?"

The other girl tossed the basketball in the air and let it bounce at her feet, then began dribbling it. "There's more to this game than running, you know. You need a little finesse. I don't think you have it."

That Thursday afternoon, the two girls enjoyed a rare middle-of-the-week pickup game in the driveway. Track practice had been canceled and neither of them was scheduled to work. Rather than lounge around inside like they usually did, they opted to get their blood flowing with a little exercise.

The vampire's gaze was locked on the bouncing ball. "I have far more finesse than you think."

"Oh, really? Because I believe I was the one who taught

you this game in the first place." Her sister faked left and Vickie fell for it. She stumbled while Alexis juked to her right and targeted the hoop. She bounced the basketball off the backboard and through the net, a perfect layup. "How fast did you say you can run? Because this ten-minute-miler actually left you in her dust."

She scowled at her. It was fun to do a little harmless trash talking, but she was also very competitive and didn't like that she'd been duped like that.

As the other girl jogged back to the line in the pavement directly in line with the house—considered their unofficial "half-court" line—the vampire froze. Her stomach twisted, and her senses heightened. She could hear a deer scramble through the field behind the house and smelled a loaf of bread baking in Wendell's oven, two houses down the block.

Goosebumps pricked her skin and she shivered involuntarily. *Something is wrong again. Why do I feel like this? What is happening?*

The identical feeling had manifested only a few days earlier but since then, it had subsided. She'd assumed it was merely a false alarm as it usually remained consistent if there really was an issue.

"Vickie!"

Startled, she snapped back to reality. Alexis held her palms up in confusion.

"What? I'm here. Where's the basketball?"

Her sister pointed to the ball, which now rolled down the driveway. "I said, make it, take it. It's still my turn but you have to check the ball to me. Where's your head?"

She shook off the distraction and turned to retrieve the

ball, but the cover-up wasn't very convincing. "Nowhere. My head is fine. So is the rest of my body. I got a little tired there, that's all."

With her arms folded, Alexis watched skeptically as the vampire jogged down the driveway after the ball. *Something is bothering her. Give her time, though. She'll come around to telling you eventually. Don't push her.*

Once she had the ball back, she tried another juke. This time, Vickie was prepared for it and matched her step for step. She rolled to the right, took a jump shot, and barely got it out of her hands before her opponent could block it. The ball sailed toward the hoop and she smiled as she waited for it to go in.

Instead, it rolled around the rim and fell without going through. After the first bounce, Vickie surged in to make the rebound and dribbled it up the driveway to the half-court line.

She was steps away from it when her stomach twisted again. Her instinctive grunt was audible.

"Seriously, are you okay?" The other girl was really anxious now. "You don't look too hot. Something's on your mind."

"No, I'm fine. Really." She kept her gaze trained on the pavement, gritted her teeth, and tried to ignore both the pain and whatever it symbolized. "Quit going easy on me or I'll make you regret it."

With a broad smile of relief on her face, Alexis ran forward and cut her off before she could take another step. She stopped dribbling and as she raised her arms to take the shot, her muscles clenched. Inadvertently, she flung the basketball with such power that it wasn't even visible.

A loud bang resounded in the shocked silence.

The vampire stood back with a spooked look on her face. Her sister turned to see what the noise was and realized that the girl had hurled the ball with her super-strength. Instead of sailing to the hoop, it fired like a bullet into the closed garage door.

"Whoa!" Alexis jogged over to survey the damage. The white door had a huge crack in one of its panels, and the basketball was a sad, flat rubber disc. It had obviously popped on impact. She ran her fingers through her hair and picked up what was left of the ball. "I thought you said you had this under control. What happened?"

"I'm so sorry. I'll pay for a new ball out of my money. I promise."

But her sister couldn't have cared less about the ball. "I want to know that you're okay. Is something bothering you so much that you lose control of your emotions?"

"Yes, but I don't know what." She sat on the wooden frame surrounding the flower bed in the back. Her foot tapped nervously. "I feel that presence again—the one more powerful and more dangerous than the Circle."

Now definitely worried, Alexis dropped the flattened ball in the driveway and walked over to her. "I forgot all about that."

"I did too." Vickie stared at her feet. "But there is a presence. It's not here, but it's nearby. We'll come in contact with it and we will have no choice."

"What if we moved you?" The other girl shrugged. "A different part of the city or the state or maybe even a different part of the world. What do you say?"

She looked up. "Trying to get rid of me, eh?"

"No, it's not that." Alexis sat on the grass in front of her. "I want you to be safe, that's all. We can hide you somewhere."

"First of all, I'm building a life here. I don't want to simply leave my friends and my boyfriend and go somewhere else." She didn't sound romantic when she said that, but in that moment, she was only focused on staying safe.

"I know that part would be hard, but—"

"No buts. I won't go. Besides, the Circle was made up of normal guys with a special sword and they still found me from Austria. Then they found out where I lived. It's not difficult. If I moved somewhere else, someone would be able to find me."

The answer frustrated Alexis. *There is no winning with this girl.* "Then what do you want to do? You can't keep doing all this. You can't break things every other week, and you can't use your powers in public anyway. I really don't know how to handle this."

"I don't know either. But that's my fight, not yours. I need to know how to handle it."

Vickie stood and, without another word, walked around the pool and to the patch of remaining yard to stare out at the large basin. *Something is out there. Something is pulling me in. But I won't take that bait until I know what it is.*

Her sister followed and stood beside her. "What are you thinking about?"

"There's something out there." She pointed to the basin. "I can't put my finger on it, but something is out there looking to kill me."

The news made the other girl uncomfortable. *You'd*

think after seeing attempts on her life over the past year that I would be desensitized to it. But it still bothers me. "Do you want to go out there and see it for yourself?"

"No. I'd really rather not."

———

That evening, after dinner, the girls sat down to do their homework in their respective rooms. Soon, everyone was asleep.

Except for Vickie.

She tossed and turned and clutched her stomach. Sweat rolled down the side of her face and soaked into the pillow beneath her head. Her jaw clenched and her eyes squeezed tightly shut. *I need to know what this is. I can't do it like this anymore.*

Finally, she sat up in her bed and took deep breaths to try to calm herself. And while her nerves were still jittery, she could at least stop shaking and trembling so violently.

I need to know what's going on. I can't spend the rest of my life wondering. Who knows when this would go away? It's time to investigate.

But as she lowered her feet to the floor, she remembered that she wasn't allowed to use her powers. No one was in grave danger, so she wouldn't be able to justify it.

If you run into anyone, tell them you're going for a walk.

Soon, she emerged quietly from her bedroom dressed all in black—a concerted effort to not be seen if at all possible.

To her relief, Craig had turned in early that night. She wouldn't have to make any excuses to him. She tiptoed to the side door and stepped through to the outside world again.

Vickie glanced at the house several times while she walked down the driveway and around the pool. She wanted to be sure no lights turned on to indicate that someone was awake.

Once she reached the same position in front of the field again, she closed her eyes and took a few deep, measured breaths. *Whatever you do, don't get caught.*

She hoped that all this was merely her vampire instincts worked up and that there was no real threat. Still, she was committed to at least investigate and she released her super-speed to race down the hill and into the basin of the field. Seconds later, she was across the hollow area and stood at the edge of the forest on the far side.

Once she stopped, her legs burned a little. *Man, it feels good to put on that kind of speed again. Whew!* To her dismay, her stomach was still in knots. *This is a threat. It's the real thing. Otherwise, that run would have helped me calm.*

Her instincts demanded that she listen to them so she walked slowly into the field again and searched for any clues. *The feeling is definitely coming from here. It has to be. It's too strong.*

The farther she walked, the more intense the feeling became. She swiveled her head constantly to look around to see if anyone was watching her. Despite the internal warnings and anxiety, she sensed that she was alone, so it was okay.

Finally, she felt drawn in a particular direction. Vickie sneered as she followed it. *I'm close to where I was surrounded by the Circle. Who knows? Maybe I'd be buried out here if what they planned had happened.*

To her surprise, she found a large rectangle of dirt that had clearly been filled recently. It was where Jim Trembo and the other government agents had dug although she wasn't aware of what exactly they'd done or who they were. *It already looks like someone has been buried here. Weird.*

She stepped closer to the mound of dirt, which was only slightly flattened. *Am I being drawn here for some kind of symbolism? Why am I led to a place I've already been? There's nothing out here. How can this place be a threat?*

Still, she couldn't deny her instincts. A rush of adrenaline coursed through her veins. A little confused, she chalked it up to reflexive response to the site of a threat versus the site of a previous encounter.

Vickie turned to head to the house but looked back. *If my system is going this haywire, there has to be something here.*

Not interested in clawing through dirt and without a shovel in her hand, Vickie did not dig out the area. While she walked into the house, however, she continued to be preoccupied with that strong, undeniable feeling of dread that kicked in while she stood at that dirt pile.

CHAPTER SIX

Vickie yawned as she stepped out of the locker room and onto the gym floor, tugging at the drawstring on her gym shorts.

"Rough night?" Krista smirked at her while she pulled her elbow to stretch her arms in anticipation of the class's activities.

She blinked a few times to try to clear the scratchiness. "I haven't been sleeping well lately. It's catching up to me, I guess." She had no idea why, but her instincts had repeatedly nagged at her. A sense of impending doom hung over her head wherever she went, which made it almost impossible to relax.

At the far end of the gym stood a diminutive middle-aged woman with close-cropped hair and a seemingly permanent smile filled with prominent, blazing-white teeth. She wore a navy-blue polo shirt with a red-and-white CL stitched over the breast, gray eighties-style short shorts, and bright white sneakers.

The woman was the exact opposite of Vickie in that

moment and practically bounced on her heels with bubbly energy. Obviously, she was ready for the day's activities and couldn't wait to share them with the class.

"All right, people, let's bring it in." She clapped her hands with excitement while the students all dragged their feet like zombies and slouched closer to her.

Gym class was always divided into two sections. For half the semester, the students learned different sports and how to play them, from hockey to pickleball. In the second half, the curriculum changed to health and nutrition.

Out were golf swings. In were food pyramids.

Out were foot races. In were pushups and sit-ups.

Out were volleyball serves. In were calories, carbs, and fiber.

The leader of this portion of the semester was Ms Mary Marozick, a chipper teacher who made no secret about the fact that she loved her job and its subject matter. Although this type of energy was normally infectious, Ms Marozick's cheerful attitude somehow made the students even slower and more lethargic.

She ushered them all to sit in front of her in a half-circle on the shiny wood floor of the gym. Some sat with their legs crossed, while others laid down and propped themselves up by their elbows. Vickie hugged her knees to stay upright, although all she wanted was to lay down and drift off to sleep for a few minutes.

"Today is a special day," the teacher announced to the class. "The end of the year is fast approaching, and that means it is time for group projects." An audible groan rippled through the class, and she met it with an amused smile. "Oh, it's not so bad. Hey, we'll only deal with useful topics—things that apply to everyone."

Toward the back of the room, Krista buried her face in her hands. "I hate group projects so much. Every time I get into a group, I wind up doing most of the work myself. It drives me up the wall."

The vampire hadn't participated in group projects related to actual classes, so she looked forward to the opportunity. "At least it mixes it up a little." She adopted an encouraging tone, although Krista failed to connect with the sentiment. "I'll make sure I carry my weight. We'll do it together so you won't have to worry about doing all the work."

The other girl knew better than to hope for such an impossible set of circumstances. *I guess she'll have to find out for herself.*

"You'll be divided into groups of four." Ms Marozick leafed through a stack of worksheets cradled in her right arm and licked her thumb constantly so she could separate the sticky sheets. "Everyone, take a sheet and pass it around. These are the guidelines for the project, and there's a place for you to take notes. Since this is gym class, I assume none of you have pens on you."

The students all looked at each other, bewildered. No one had ever been asked to bring a pen to gym class. She nodded and handed out a bundle of pens held together with a rubber band.

As they passed around the stack of papers, each student took one sheet, while the teacher paced slowly in front of them, her hands folded behind her back. "Each of you will give a presentation on a certain aspect of daily health. This is intended to be a useful presentation—which means I don't want you to simply parrot facts about diet and exercise or whatever. Your job as a team will be to put together an interesting, exciting, and applicable presentation on the subject matter I will assign to you. This is supposed to be useful for your everyday life, not merely what it says in some textbook or encyclopedia."

Several students snickered at the thought of anyone using an encyclopedia. A few of the slower students looked confused as to what an encyclopedia even was.

Everyone processed the news with varying degrees of despondency but Vickie was not fazed. *I think Krista and I could put together a good presentation for the class. We seem to have good chemistry, and it would be fun to work together.*

As she held onto her optimism, Ms Marozick lowered the boom—twice.

"You will work in groups of four, and I will assign each of you to a group. Then, you will give the presentation in front of the entire student body."

Vickie's stomach sank. *I won't get to choose who to work with? Man. That sucks.*

Jaws dropped across the assembled group of students. One raised her hand. "Why will we present in front of the whole school? What's the point?"

Like she did with anything anyone said to her, the teacher responded with a large, toothy smile. "We're trying something new this year. There is a concern among many adults that kids do not establish healthy lifestyle choices. The teachers met to discuss the issue, and we agreed that a series of assemblies on the matter would be best. But we didn't think that only a number of assemblies would be enough. Studies have shown that everyone listens more intently when they receive advice from a peer, so our gym class will present the guidelines for healthy living to the student body. Then, we can count it as an assignment and it can be a part of your grade." The enthusiasm in her voice as she relayed the news was in stark contrast to the thousand-yard stares that the students gave her in response.

No one knew how to handle it. No other class had been forced to give presentations in front of the school. This was new territory.

Vickie was bummed. *I really hoped to do this with Krista. She's the only one who has been really nice to me in this class. Maybe I'll be put with her anyway.*

Her hopes were soon dashed as the teacher paced once again with a clipboard in front of her and announced the groups.

One by one, students hung their heads as they heard their team assignments. A scant few made excited eye contact, knowing they would present with their friends, but the others sighed and their expressions were glum.

The vampire felt much the same when she heard her name and not Krista's.

"Then, we have Vickie Hewitt, Adam Thiele, Sam Trissel, and Emily Zimmerman."

The woman's voice rambled on while Vickie processed her group assignments.

She glanced at Adam Thiele, who leaned back on his palms with an unimpressed look on his face. *I don't know Adam, but he strikes me as a little cocky. And that bleached-blonde spiked hair is weird. I don't know why someone would choose to look like that. And what is the purpose of that huge studded bracelet strapped to his wrist? He was one of the loudest people who made fun of me earlier this semester. I'm not looking forward to working with him.*

Then, she scanned the students until she saw Emily and Sam. *He seems nice. So does Emily. She is at least a smart girl. She didn't participate in all the stupid mocking the other girls did, but she did laugh a lot. I don't know how to feel about any of this. Will they share the work or will I be stuck leading the way?*

Before she could even think about an answer, the teacher spoke again. "Now that you all have your group assignments, I want you to huddle up. We'll select topics." She smiled again and looked as though she'd announced that ice cream and pizza would be handed out, not topics for a huge group project no one wanted to do.

The vampire walked reluctantly to the general area where her group members were all seated. Adam didn't look at her. Sam glanced awkwardly at her, and Emily smiled politely. Vickie nodded to them but no one spoke.

Ms Marozick dropped her clipboard and picked up a small wicker basket that contained folded pieces of paper. Practically giddy with suppressed excitement, she shook the basket as she walked from group to group and instructed them to draw their subject.

One by one, each group made their selections. Some students pumped their fist and laughed at whatever they had chosen. A few curled their lips in disgust and sneered at the paper with their topic.

When the teacher arrived at their group, Emily stood and took a piece of paper. Adam finally spun on his butt to face the group and waited for her to announce what they had drawn.

"We have *Jogging and Running as a Daily Practice*." The girl raised her eyebrows and nodded. "It's not the worst subject, I guess."

Adam didn't seem very excited about it. "Yippee."

Sam pointed to Vickie. "Hey, at least we have the star runner here."

"What?" She sent him a confused look.

"Come on, this should be a topic you could handle in your sleep." He pushed his glasses up the bridge of his nose. "You run all the time. We can have you talk about it for a few minutes and we'll be out the door."

It was a joke, obviously, and everyone chuckled. Still, she began to feel very nervous about the whole thing.

Why am I scared? It's not like anything bad would happen to me. What's the worst that could happen? I get a little nervous? I say something wrong? No one will harm me. I don't understand why something like this would make me so nervous.

But she was. She closed her eyes for a moment and imagined herself on stage, speaking to the entire student body. Her stomach twisted into knots—not the same feeling she had when under the threat of physical harm, but a new kind of nervousness she hadn't felt before.

For the first time in her life, she was worried about being embarrassed.

CHAPTER SEVEN

The students all milled about and their nervous but excited footsteps bounced off the hard wood floor and lingered in the choir room.

Jess and Jamie swapped jokes about what class they should be in as they looked at the clock.

"How ironic that it's a day off and we're still at school?" Jess shook her head, amused.

"At least we're excited to be at school this time." She continued her record of attempting to be positive at every opportunity.

A somewhat anxious Alexis unhooked the bottom loop of the hanging case that contained her choir robe and unzipped it while she held the robe up by the hanger. *I didn't forget my stole, did I? Mr Goede will freak out if I did. If I'm the only one representing our school who doesn't have a stole on her robe, I'll look like an idiot.*

To her relief, the shiny blue-and-white stole hung like a perfect triangle around the neck of her bright blue choir robe. She was safe this time.

"Okay, everyone!" Mr Goede shouted as he marched into the choir room and dodged suitcases and duffel bags en route to the front. The students quieted and turned their attention to him. "The bus is at the back exit right now, and we'll board very soon. Now, I know for some of you, this is your first ChoralFest. It's a fun weekend that so many of us look forward to, but please remember a few rules you need to follow."

Their attention drifted in and out as he rattled off guidelines about what time to be where and punishments for missing deadlines—the usual fare for a group of high school kids.

He produced a stack of goldenrod-colored papers and began to hand them out. "Take one and pass the stacks around. These are your schedules for the entire weekend. Do not lose these. I expect you to be on your best behavior, and that means adhering to this schedule."

Alexis took one and scanned it briefly, knowing she would have more than enough time to digest it on the bus.

The principal folded his hands and brought them to his chest. "Unfortunately, we've had to institute a new rule on this trip due to incidents from last year which we will not discuss. From here on, everyone will be required to sit boy-boy or girl-girl on the bus. There will be no boy-girl pairings. If you have a boyfriend or a girlfriend in choir, you will not be able to sit with them." A collective groan issued from the group. "Yes, well…sometimes, a few bad apples ruin the whole bushel."

She paused to contemplate the expression, not entirely sure what it meant, when she caught Charlie glancing at her with a smile. They locked gazes for a second, exchanged awkward smirks, and turned away.

Jess leaned in and nudged her with her elbow. "So much for a little romance on the bus, eh?"

"Shut up." She frowned. "Like we were even going to sit together. He would probably have sat with his friends anyway like I'm sitting with you guys."

Mr Goede continued. "Okay, okay, quiet now. The bus will take us directly to the high school, and we will meet with our host families and separate for the evening. Do you have any questions?"

One girl raised her hand. "How long a drive is it?"

"Good question. From here to Onalaska is about three hours."

I love that name. Alexis double-checked her duffel bag one more time. *Like, how does Wisconsin have so many weird names based on other places? Rome, New Berlin...but Onalaska is so dumb. Can't they simply call it Alaska? Laziness at its finest.*

"Please be at the bus in five minutes so that you can load your bags and we can get going." The principal gestured with his arms to usher the group forward and slipped ahead of them to exit the room.

She hoisted her bag onto her shoulder and sighed. As she didn't want to hold her robe up over her head to keep it from dragging on the floor, she hooked the bottom loop to the hanger to fold it in half and draped it over her duffel bag so that her hands could be free.

Charlie tapped her on the shoulder before she moved to the door. She spun to where he stood calmly with his hands stuck in his pockets. "Bummer about the new rule, hey?" he said.

"Oh, yeah." She smiled politely and pretended to fumble with the zipper on her bag as if she had something else to do. *Why are you doing this? Act like a normal human being. He doesn't care if you look cool or not.* "Were you thinking of sitting with me?"

He flashed the smile that sent shockwaves through her. "Yeah, why not? I thought it would be fun to chill together for a few hours. But I guess I understand why. I heard about Megan Haaken and Rich Bocchini last year." He tilted his head and his face twisted in skepticism. "I don't think anyone else would be that stupid, honestly. On a bus full of people?"

"Seriously." She had heard whisperings of what happened a few times but not enough to really understand what had taken place on the bus last year. She only knew it was bad and that was enough for her.

"I'm sure we'll have some time to hang out, though." He sounded optimistic and held his itinerary up. "It looks like there's a dance on Saturday night. Maybe save me a few dances?"

"A few? I'll save you all the dances." Alexis laughed, although her brain didn't find the comment funny. *Wow, that was lame. You better hope he laughs at that or you're dead in the water.*

To her relief, Charlie snickered at the comment, his smile sincere. "Thanks. See? We'll at least have that. There will be breaks and stuff. We'll be able to hang."

One of his buddies slapped him on the shoulder as he

walked out of the room. He followed, his thumbs tucked behind the straps of his backpack.

Alexis was suddenly much angrier at the new seating rule than she had been when she first heard it. *Really? He wanted to sit with you? And now he can't?* She cursed Megan and Rich silently for ruining it for everyone.

For the next three hours, she sat with Jess on the bus, swapped stories, snuck in short naps, and wondered aloud how the weekend would go.

"How many schools will be at this event?" She stared at the itinerary.

"It's like a dozen or something." Her friend stared out the window. "I hear the combined choirs always sound amazing."

As she ran her finger down the goldenrod sheet, Alexis pointed out the separate performances on Saturday afternoon, along with the group performances on Sunday afternoon. "That's a ton of singing. Will we even be ready to sing together by Sunday? That's only two days away, and we're not even in town yet."

It didn't seem to bother Jess, who rested her head against the seat and closed her eyes. "They must be able to put it together quickly enough." She yawned. "Otherwise, they wouldn't do this every year."

The bus rumbled on. Alexis pulled her Kindle out of her bag and read for about an hour in an effort to pass the time. During slow parts of the book, she daydreamed about sitting beside Charlie for the three hours, laughing and nudging each other playfully and trying to flirt. She would have been nervous but she would also have had a good time.

A quick glance down the aisle of the bus revealed the back of his head while he laughed with one of his buddies. She cracked a disappointed half-smile. *Oh, well. We'll find a way to make this weekend fun for us both.*

They arrived in Onalaska at 11:00 am and the bus rumbled to a stop in a line of others in front of the school at the edge of a full parking lot.

"Jeez, it looks like a school day for them or something." Jess squinted through the glass at car after car that filled the space in front of them.

Mr Goede pulled himself to his feet and walked to the front of the bus. "I know it looks like there is school going on right now, but inside there are other schools getting situated and meeting their host families as well. It's very crowded in there. That's why it is important for you to follow directions this morning. We will walk through those doors and head directly to the gym. There will be a section marked off for our school there. Let's find that and we can then meet up with host families and get separated for the afternoon."

A boy raised his hand. "Will we get to eat lunch?"

The principal nodded. "Your host families will provide lunch for you. The sooner we get into the gym, the sooner you meet your hosts and the sooner you will get lunch. Let's go, people."

He turned, stepped off the bus, and walked excitedly to the school entrance. One by one, each student disembarked and retrieved their bag from the curb on their way in once chaperones had removed the luggage from the storage compartment under the vehicle.

Jamie met up with the two girls and the three of them

walked to the main doors. "I hope we have a good host family. It would be a huge bummer if we were stuck with some boring family where we have nothing to do."

Alexis ignored the comment and instead, focused on the huge overhang that extended from the entrance. "Man, this school must have money. You could line up three cars wide under this roof. It's like the entrance to a big hotel or convention center."

"It's a country school." Jess nodded and studied the portico herself. "People out here have money, so private high schools are a little nicer. We're in the city and don't make nearly as much money as families out here do."

They wove through the crowd of students, all decked out in their own school's letterman jackets, and the girls enjoyed the view—purple jackets, red jackets, blue jackets, and black jackets. It was a reminder of how big the world really was, even though this was merely a handful of schools in the Midwest.

In her mind, Alexis was a little disappointed by the newly built school building and gym. *Everything is so shiny and fresh. It feels modern in here. There isn't enough of this at Clear Lake. It makes me feel like we're behind the times or something.*

She also wanted to catch up to Charlie, but he had gone on ahead and was already halfway across the gym before they reached the double doors leading to the open space. Once the girls walked in, they saw a huge banner with *CLEAR LAKE HIGH SCHOOL* emblazoned in red, white, and blue lettering to match the school colors. Clearly, the students at the Onalaska High School had made banners for each school. It was a nice personal touch.

The students were corraled together and introduced to their hosts as Mr Goede walked from family to family, greeted them, and pointed them toward the students they would host. Jess, Jamie, and Alexis stood together and waited for their hosts to arrive.

Soon, a middle-aged couple greeted them. The husband, with balding curly hair and glasses, wore a stoic but polite expression. His wife smiled broadly and excitedly as she stepped forward, her white hair shining against the overhead lights.

"Girls? I'm Connie Bader, and this is my husband, Bill." The man waved. "We're your hosts for the next few nights. Come on, we have a van out front and we'll take you to our house to drop your bags off and get settled."

CHAPTER EIGHT

Vickie blinked a few times, stretched her arms out over her head, and sat up in her bed. The sunlight peeked through the blinds and fought its way into the room to throw illuminating stripes on her bed.

Days off always threw her for a loop. *It's Friday but it feels like Saturday. I don't have to work and I don't have to go to school. I won't know what to do with myself today.*

She swung her feet over the edge of her bed and planted them on the floor but immediately registered a sense of discomfort. *There is still something happening.* She placed her hand on her stomach. *This pinching feeling won't go away, no matter what I do. It's like I get these waves where I freak out, but when they disappear, what's left is still this feeling that something is wrong. I don't know what, though.*

Despite the nagging feeling, she was determined to enjoy her day off. She rose to her feet and shuffled out into the hallway. The night before, she'd thought she would sleep until nine or ten am, but when she looked at the clock on the wall in the kitchen, she was disappointed to see it was only seven-thirty. *So much for sleeping in. I guess my body is so used to getting up before six that this is the latest I'll sleep. Oh, well.*

The house was distractingly quiet. Alexis was on her way to ChoralFest. Her father had dropped her off at the school, so he wouldn't be home for a while. Between the silence and the feeling in her gut, she very quickly felt the urge to fill the void in the house and distract herself.

The vampire moved to the living room and located the remote to turn the TV on. After she'd scrolled through a few options, she landed on HGTV and selected an episode of *House Hunters.* A couple in Denver was searching for a large home in the city.

Perfect. Something distracting but not too thought-provoking. She plopped in the recliner. *This show is so ridiculous. I haven't been in this century for a year and even I know you won't find a big house in the city. You folks better start looking at the suburbs.*

During the first commercial break, she felt a different twinge in her stomach—hunger. She stood and wandered into the kitchen to find breakfast. As she strolled past the large sliding glass door facing the back yard, she stopped in her tracks.

Her stomach twisted again and this time, it wasn't hunger. *What is happening? Come on, body, can't you tell me what's going on instead of going through all this nonsense?* Of course, her body didn't reply.

Vickie looked out the window and saw a bright, sunny day. She really wanted to enjoy it. *I hope this is only a threat of something bad happening to someone else. I can't do anything about that anyway. I simply want to have a nice day off.*

She settled on cereal for breakfast as she didn't want to spend time cooking that morning. Her decision made, she retrieved a bowl from the kitchen cupboard and a box of Fruity Pebbles from the pantry cupboard.

Whoever thought of putting food in a bowl and pouring milk over the top of it? She smirked while she poured the rainbow-colored cereal into the bowl. *This stuff is so good. I wish I had this growing up.*

Once she'd filled the bowl halfway with milk, she retrieved a spoon and carried her breakfast to the living room in time to catch the show returning from its commercial break. With the bowl in one hand and the spoon in the other, she pushed the cereal into the milk with the back end of the spoon. The liquid was already turning from white to a pinkish hue.

Even though her body told her something was wrong, she was surprisingly relaxed. *Now, this is the life. No farming, no hunting, no shopping. Only something good to watch and easily accessible food. I never get to enjoy days off like this.*

It was true. Her free time on the weekends was generally filled with activity, whether that was doing chores around the house at Craig's request or working a shift at the seafood place. She savored the opportunity to just do nothing.

Out in the field behind the house, Jim Trembo, Pete Stabone, and the team trudged along and headed to the area in the field where they had discovered the sword and the blood samples.

"Help me out here, Jim." Pete scowled as he walked. "We've already dug this area. We've pulled a ton of information that will lead to where we want to go with this investigation. Why are we back out here again?"

"We'll fan out a little farther." Jim's tone of voice was a little on the exasperated side. Things had gone so well, he didn't feel he needed to explain himself. Everything required further investigation. "I want to see if we can find any clues that will tie us to the high school."

In his mind, there was enough sloppiness in the evidence left behind that he felt there could be more out in that field. *The girl in the video didn't try to hide her shirt, even though it was a dead giveaway. The sword is massive, yet it was left behind. There must be more in this field that we can use to point us towards the identity of this being.*

The crew shared Pete's sentiments and felt they had exhausted the evidence in that field. Regardless, they followed orders and soon, they crawled on their hands and knees to inspect the area carefully.

"We're looking for anything here, boys." Jim folded his arms and stood over them. "You find a strand of hair? I want to know about it. The same goes for clothing fibers, even a discolored blade of grass. Leave nothing unturned on this."

When he heard these orders, Pete pushed himself to his feet and pulled him aside. "Aren't you worried that you've become a little obsessive? There must be other paths we can explore. Why aren't you at the high school trying to get in there? I thought that was the next step."

He shook his head. "The school is closed today. I can't do anything with that plan until next week. But I want to be prepared and I'm not obsessed. I'm only trying to cover every detail. And shoot, what else should I do—spend the next three days twiddling my thumbs? We have a whole day to make progress. That's why we're here."

His companion waved his arm and gestured at the row of houses in the distance. "Jim, this creature could be anywhere. I don't think we'll find much evidence here anyway. If we believe this supernatural activity is coming from someone at Clear Lake High School, we ought to simply take the day off, prep ourselves, and be ready to go there on Monday morning to get in. We're wasting time and energy."

Jim followed his gesture to the houses and took a few steps in that direction while he stared silently at each home. Behind him, Pete stood with his hands on his hips and shook his head.

"Are you even listening to me right now, Jim?"

Inside the house, Vickie had finished her bowl of cereal but while her hunger was satisfied, her instincts had begun to go crazy. In an effort to shake it off, she stood and carried the bowl and spoon into the kitchen, where she placed them in the sink.

As she walked across the kitchen, she stopped again in front of the glass door. This time, she looked out into the field where a small group of men crawled around the area where she had fought with the Circle.

Her stomach dropped. *That's them. That's whoever I'm*

sensing. But it looks like the group of guys I saw there once before. What's the threat?

It unsettled her that they appeared to be engaged in a close search of the area where she'd had her altercation. Worse, though, was the two men a few yards away from the group who stood in the middle of the field. One of them was motionless and stared in her direction. *He can't see me, can he?*

For safety's sake, she slid past the door and up against the wall before she peered carefully around the corner. She squinted and tried to have a good look at him. Unfortunately, her powers did not allow her the ability to see from that great a distance.

My senses are heightened but he's too far away. I can't get a read on him. The only thing I can sense is that he is bad news.

For a few brief moments, the two of them stared at where the other was even though neither could see anyone closely. A connection hung in the air while they both stood motionless.

"Guys, Pete's right." Jim turned away from the row of houses. "Let's take the day off. We won't get anywhere with this today. Instead, we'll regroup, and you guys can hang out on call while we put our plan together to get into the high school."

A rush of relief swept the men who seemed satisfied now that they didn't have to dig meticulously into each possible clue in the field all day long.

Pete patted the other man on the shoulder. "Atta boy.

It's the right call. The last thing you need is to push these guys into mutiny."

"I merely have an overwhelming sense that we have the information we need." Jim faced the houses again. "The girl is out there and we can find her in the high school. We don't need anything else from here."

"I sure wish you had realized that before you made us all come out here." His companion chuckled while the men fell in behind him. "We could have saved considerable effort."

"Yeah, you're right, and I apologize." He turned to the men. "But there's no blueprint on how to do this. This is the farthest we've come before, guys. I'm figuring this out as I go along."

The group began to walk across the field and back to their cars. He stopped again and stared at the houses. *You're out there. I know you are.*

Inside, Vickie walked cautiously to the living room. Another episode of *House Hunters* was on the TV but she couldn't enjoy it. She sat in a funk, distracted by what she had seen in the field.

Craig walked in on his return from dropping his daughter off at school. "Hey, you're up!" he announced as he entered. "Alexis is on her way to Onalaska, and it's only us this weekend—are you okay? You look like you've seen a ghost or something."

"I don't know what I've seen. But it's not good."

CHAPTER NINE

Alexis climbed out of the red minivan, her black leather music folder clutched tightly against her chest. She waved to Connie and joined the rest of the girls on their way into the school under the impressive portico.

So far, things had gone well. Their hosts had taken them to their house to drop their bags. To their delight, each girl had their own sleeping space. The Bader Family had two daughters away at college, so there were two bedrooms open. The third girl—who wound up being Alexis in this case—got to sleep on a surprisingly comfortable pull-out couch in the finished basement.

Once they were situated, Connie took them all out to McDonald's for lunch and finally satisfied Alexis' hunger pangs. For about forty-five minutes, they got to know the woman, who was an art teacher at the school. She was bright, funny, and very warm. The girls were immediately comfortable with her.

Now that lunch was over, however, it was time to put in a little work. ChoralFest was known for two things—an abundance of singing and fun with your friends for the weekend.

When the girls walked into the school lobby, several teachers from the schools directed foot traffic, including Mrs Schram, one of the directors from Clear Lake. She smiled at the girls and waved them down the hall like she was a third-base coach signaling for the runner to head to home base.

The girls giggled at her and followed instructions. "She's such a goofball." Alexis shook her head.

"I think that's her charm." Jamie again offered the positive outlook. "Would you rather spend a weekend dealing with her or with Mr Goede?"

Her friends shuddered. "Her. Definitely." Alexis looked over her shoulder at them. "But that's not an option this weekend."

They reached the door to a practice room. When they peeked in, they saw a few Clear Lake students amongst the others which confirmed that it was the right place to be. Not knowing where to sit, they simply walked inside and leaned against the wall while they waited for further instructions.

The room was impressive. Black chairs fanned out in a half-circle around a wooden riser in the middle, which held a music stand. The chairs were on risers as well to create theater-like seating for the choir. The space itself was massive and large enough to hold three different choirs in one place. Various musical instruments were piled against the far wall.

"No wonder this place is so big," Alexis observed. "It must be the band room."

"It's still bigger than our band room," Jess added. "Sometimes, I feel like high school is a big deal, and then I go to other high schools and see how big it really could be."

Jamie laughed. "I know. It's like going to Chicago. Downtown Milwaukee is big, but Chicago makes it feel like a village by comparison."

A tall, slender man with curly black hair and small round eyeglasses breezed in and headed to the riser in the middle. He placed a large burgundy binder onto the music stand and pushed gently to lower it to about waist level so he could see in all directions.

"Okay, everyone. It's time to take your seats." He pointed to the rows of chairs to instruct them so all the bass singers were in one row, all the tenors in another, and on down to the altos and the sopranos.

The singers arranged themselves into groups based on their schools. As it was early in the weekend, very few of them intermingled unless they specifically knew someone, which was the exception rather than the rule. Alexis sat with Jess and Jamie, where she was comfortable.

The students settled and she noticed Charlie break off from his friends and urge all the singers to move down in the row ahead of them. He approached the chair directly in front of Alexis, smiled at her, and sat.

He'd rather sit in front of me than with his buddies? Her cheeks flushed while Jess elbowed her again and snickered.

"Is everyone in place? We're all settled in? Good!" The man stood with his arms dangling at his sides and he smiled at them. "My name is Mr Levy. I will be the director of this portion of the combined choirs. Many of you already know this, but the choirs here at ChoralFest are divided into three groups. We will sing a few selections ourselves, and so will each of the other groups. Also, we will sing together in one unified choir to open and close Sunday's concert. Now, we have a considerable amount to get through and master over the course of the next couple of days, so please take this music and pass it around. This will be our opening number for our portion of the concert."

The piles made their way through the rows until they reached Alexis. She was excited when she recognized the title—*"This Is Me" from the Major Motion Picture, The Greatest Showman.*

"Sweet," Jamie whispered. "I love this song."

Charlie turned to Alexis. "Have you ever seen this movie?"

She leaned forward. "Are you kidding? This is one of my favorites."

"Everyone, please face forward." The teacher adopted a stern tone. "I know it's exciting to all be together here, but again, we have challenging practice ahead and not much time to do it in. I want to be really focused while we are in this room." He paced on the little riser and seemed to burst with energy but with no place to put it. "Many of you already know this song, but I want you to fight the urge to sing it like you have always done. You will fall into bad habits and probably sing it improperly. We'll take this a piece at a time, a part at a time, and we will be very careful. I promise you, if you follow my directions and sing it the way I insist, it will come together impressively and the audience will love it—and you will love it too."

Alexis tapped her foot in excitement. She was already

enjoying herself at her first ChoralFest. *Jeez, in our choir, we sing boring songs like "Send In The Clowns" or whatever. This is a fun one.*

One by one, each section of the choir rehearsed the first stanza of the song. To the girls, it sounded weird to hear the song broken into parts as they obviously hadn't done that in the movie. Similarly, there was no solo in this version, as the first verse was divided into the female section of the choir.

Mr Levy told them to sing it through together to the chorus as if they were performing it on Sunday.

The sopranos started.

I am not a stranger to the dark

Hide away, they say

'Cause we don't want your broken parts

The altos picked it up.

I've learned to be ashamed of my scars

Run away, they say

No one'll love you as you are

The girls joined together in the lead-up to the chorus.

But I won't let them break me down to dust...

By the time they reached the phrase, *"For we are glorious,"* the girls had swelled into a beautiful surge of energy, more than was necessary for that point in the song, but the group couldn't help themselves.

The boys joined the chorus. The group continued to increase in volume and almost burst with excited energy as they reached the crescendo of the song—*"I am who I'm meant to be, this is me!"*

They continued to sing and the teacher allowed it although they hadn't practiced the next section yet. The choir built in ferocity and confidence as most of them were very familiar with the song.

He finally raised his hands with a broad smile and stopped them when they reached the post-chorus chants of "*Oh-oh-oh-ohhhhhhh.*"

The group burst into applause and laughter. Chills ran up the spines of several of the singers, including Alexis. "That was awesome." She practically shouted the approval.

Charlie turned and laughed. "It sounds even better than the movie."

Mr Levy raised his palms to calm them. "Okay, okay. I let you go a little farther this time for two reasons. First, you all sounded really good and I wanted to hear it." Everyone laughed. "But also, I wanted you to really feel the music and I could tell that you were. Many of us are in choir to get an easy credit or whatever, but this song is easy to become emotionally invested in. This is fun. Choir is fun. And that's why I chose this particular song. For all its faults and flaws, *The Greatest Showman* is a fun movie. It reminds us that music can be an enjoyable experience, critics aside. We'll hammer on this song a fair amount, but don't forget that moment—and I saw it in your faces as you reached it—when you belted out '*I'm not scared to be seen, I make no apologies, This is me.*' Some of you looked ready to charge out of that door with your fists in the air."

The students laughed again as he continued. "We have to fix a fair amount of what you sang, but that energy— that belief in what you were singing—that's what I want to see from you when we put it all together. Please don't lose that because it's what will make the audience on Sunday go from 'Oh, what a lovely rendition' to 'Holy cow! I almost fell out of my chair.'"

The girls looked at each other and laughed. Charlie turned to laugh with them and shook his head.

Alexis was enjoying herself. She was away from every-thing else that had defined her school year, and she was with the people she cared about who didn't live with her.

And she was having a great time. ChoralFest was exactly what she needed although she hadn't known she needed it.

No parents, no vampires, and no grocery store. No drama and only fun, music, and friends. Boy, I could get used to this.

The group spent the next hour working hard on the song before they moved on to the next one, but the combined voices of several choirs singing at their peak together kept the energy alive in the room and it was a beautiful thing.

CHAPTER TEN

"Will you be okay?" Craig pushed the SUV into Park in front of Al's Seafood.

Vickie paused for a moment, closed her eyes, and tried to tap into her senses. "I think so. I don't feel anything dangerous in the area. Whoever that was in the field isn't nearby now. I don't feel great, but I think I'm fine."

"Well, if you need something, please call, all right?"

"You don't have a date tonight?"

"Not tonight. You need someone to pick you up. I'll have a date tomorrow night since you'll be off work then. But we'll talk about that, given the circumstances. Seriously, call me. Don't use your powers, whatever you do."

She turned to exit the vehicle. "I know, I know. It seems silly, though. If I'm in danger, you'd think you would want me to use my powers, right?"

He shook his head. "Let's treat this like you're a regular teenager and not a vampire today, okay? We both know your powers will expose you. Normal teenage girls call their parents when something is wrong. Hold off on the powers."

With a sigh, she stepped out, closed the door, and leaned in to talk through the open window. "Fine. I'll call you if something happens. But really, I feel okay right now."

"Right now, but that might change. But have a good night." He drove off and she walked around the back of the building.

The stench of fish caught her squarely in the nose once she opened the door to walk through the back of the building. She had grown used to the smell and didn't notice it nearly as powerfully as her family did whenever she returned from work.

But for some reason, the fish smell was more potent that evening and it caught her off-guard. *Stay patient today. No powers, no strength, and no speed. You're simply a normal teenage girl working a normal teenage job on a normal Friday night. That's all.*

"Happy Fish Fry Day!" Jason, her coworker, shouted as he tied an apron around his waist.

In Wisconsin, any place that served fish was usually flooded on Friday nights. It was a long-held tradition for Wisconsinites to enjoy a fish fry after a long week of work. Al's Seafood took advantage of the customer preference. It hosted an excellent fish fry, and many in the neighborhood —and outside the neighborhood—would swing past on Fridays to get their dinners.

Vickie didn't mind Friday nights. In fact, prior to this one, in particular, she enjoyed them. She requested to work in the back and did most of the grunt work that no one liked to do like dishes, unpacking boxes, cleaning, and breading fish. Because everyone was so distracted by the constant stream of customers that streamed in once the doors were unlocked, she could often tap into her powers and make short work of her duties without anyone paying attention to her.

But now that she had come too close to being revealed, she had to keep her word to Craig that she wouldn't use her powers while at work. For the first time since she started at Al's Seafood, she would have to endure an entire work shift as a normal teenager.

At first, it wasn't so bad. Friday nights meant that many people came in earlier than usual so preparation had to be done in advance to be sure that the back of the store was ready. Buns were stocked, fish was breaded, dishes were washed, and deep fryers were cleaned and functioning. There was considerable activity and many people around, so she didn't really notice initially that she wasn't using her powers.

She tried all the tricks most people used to get through boring work and sang along to the radio while she imagined herself at a dance with Eric or on stage performing herself. It helped to alleviate some of the monotony as she scrubbed dishes left from the previous evening, dunked them in a sink full of water to rinse them, and finally swished them through another to sanitize them.

The daydreaming had helped at first until the doors were unlocked.

By 5:00 pm, the store had a line that twisted and turned to fill the small customer area. Some pushed and shoved to get to the coolers on the side and snag frozen lobster tails for fancier dinners. Others lined up at the deli counter to order fresh crab salad, one of Al's Seafood's specialties.

Patti and Elena, two of Vickie's coworkers, worked the line at the fresh seafood counter and efficiently filled bags of shrimp and salmon fillets for anyone who ordered.

Jason manned the kitchen, and he kept a constant stream of breaded cod in the fryer, with fries in the other, while bag after bag of cod dinners piled up on the counter for waiting customers.

The vampire, as usual, played the go-fer role and did her best to put out metaphorical fires wherever she was needed. A couple of times, she ran out to the outside freezer to get more shrimp. She breaded more fish and opted to set up shop inside the back area of the store so she was around people and wouldn't be tempted to use her powers.

"Vickie!" Steve, her manager, shouted. "We're running out of rolls. It's a big night for cod sandwiches, apparently. Run next door and grab a box of rolls from the basement."

"Got it!" she shouted in response and hurried out of the back door.

Al's Seafood consisted of two buildings. On the left was the store itself, where customers got their food. It was where the kitchen was, and where ninety-five percent of everyone's time was spent.

Next door, however, was a small house—formerly the home of the owner of Al's Seafood, Al Thompson. After he died and his wife and son took over, the house transformed into a glorified warehouse and had become only a place to store excess inventory and surplus food.

Vickie kept her word and did not tap into her powers,

although she was already weary of running around at normal speed. To her surprise, moving at regular speed was actually more tiring than using her super-speed, at least in short bursts.

She pulled the back door of the house open and flipped the light switch to illuminate the stairs leading to the basement, which was directly in front of her.

For not the first time, she was curious about the rest of the house. *I wonder what it looked like when people lived here. Did they leave anything behind? Is there furniture inside?* To her dismay, she never really had the chance to explore since she was only sent there when they were out of something and it was an emergency. Her only task was to get the box of rolls and return to the store before customers had to wait too long.

Stacks and stacks of boxes were packed at the bottom of the stairs. Some held styrofoam cartons used for the fish dinners that went out. Others held paper bags or plastic cups. She scanned the area until she found one labeled *KAISER ROLLS.*

"Bingo," she exclaimed out loud to no one in particular.

She grasped the box, hoisted it over her head, and chuckled at how comically large it was. Despite it being only full of bread, it was surprisingly heavy. With it balanced, although a little awkwardly, she jogged to the top of the stairs but misjudged the width of the box given the way she carried it. The sudden impact into the door frame surprised her and she fell back to tumble down the stairs in a reverse somersault before her head smacked onto the tiled concrete floor.

Dazed and dizzy, she laid there for a brief second.

While she tried to regain her senses, the box of rolls dislodged a few others that landed on her face and one cracked her nose.

Vickie shoved the boxes off her and rolled to her hands and knees. Blood dripped from her nose, and a small puddle had already formed on the now cracked tile. She fumbled and felt the back of her head, which was wet as well.

I'm a mess. Holy cow, this hurts.

Still disoriented, she crawled to the steps and sat for a moment. *The only way I can get out of this in one piece is if I heal myself. I can't get in trouble for that, right? Otherwise, I'll have to go to the hospital. I can't have that.*

The vampire closed her eyes and concentrated as best she could with a dizzy head. Soon, the energy coursed through her veins and the fog lifted from her mind.

Her nose popped slightly and the pain faded, and the wound in the back of her head closed as well. Pleased with the healing, she stood to grab the box and head up the stairs again when her gaze settled on a rather large puddle of blood on the floor.

I can't leave this here or they will ask questions. There must be paper towels around here somewhere.

Carefully, she stepped over the blood and scanned box after box until she finally found a carton of paper towels toward the back of the basement. She ripped it open, yanked a roll out, and sopped up the blood at the base of the stairs.

I can't do anything about the cracked tile. Hopefully, no one will ask about that.

Once she was happy everything was suitably cleaned,

she wrapped more paper towels around the bloody ones so she wouldn't spread blood anywhere else. Then, she picked the box up and negotiated the stairs carefully and headed out the door.

On her way to the back door of the store, she detoured to the dumpster quickly to dispose of the bloody evidence and jogged into the store with the box of rolls.

"What took you so long?" Jason shouted from the kitchen. "We're drowning back here."

"Sorry. I...had trouble finding them."

"Whatever," he grumbled as he snatched the box and tore it open.

Vickie returned to washing dishes that had piled up in the back. Patti walked past her with a catfish wrapped in wax paper, ready to chop it into steaks.

"Vickie, what's with the back of your head?"

"What?"

"It's all red."

"Oh...um, I tried dyeing my hair the other day and it didn't work right. I have to fix it but I ran out of time today to do it."

Patti, with a pink streak in her hair, laughed while she retrieved one of the chef's knives from the magnet on the wall. "Next time, let me do it. I do it all the time. It's a good thing you're back here. It looks like your head was split open or something."

CHAPTER ELEVEN

In the basement of the Bader home, Alexis pulled a cardigan excitedly over her spaghetti-strap top. *It's a little chillier here than I thought it would be at this time of year.*

The weather in Onalaska—while not exactly Alaska itself—reminded them of the state's typical climate. Even though they were deep into the spring season, the girls had found themselves shivering in the breeze outside earlier after the day-long choir practice.

As the sun set on their drive back to the Bader house, temperatures plunged into the fifties and hovered at barely fifty degrees Fahrenheit.

Fortunately, the evening's activities were scheduled to be indoors—a combination of a dance party and a pool party at the local YMCA.

Before they left practice, she'd confirmed with Charlie that he wanted to dance and not swim. She crouched over the small makeup mirror balanced on the pull-out couch and dragged the eyeliner pencil over the edge of her eyelid and honestly looked forward to the festivities.

Thank goodness he said he wanted to dance. The last thing I want right now is for him to see me in a swimsuit. I'm already nervous around him. I don't know what I would do if I had to try to act casual around him in a bikini. She straightened and leaned away from the mirror to check her work. *Of course, I'm self-conscious when I dance, too. But he's seen me dance before. Our first date was the Festival dance, and he is clearly still interested. So why am I so nervous right now?*

Footsteps caught her attention and she glanced at the stairs as Jess descended into the basement. She wore a thin green pullover. "I think it's stupid that we even have to dress this warm."

"I know." Alexis turned her attention to the mirror again to add a little lip gloss to her lips. "At least I brought a cardigan so I can take it off. I'll be a sweat machine while I'm dancing."

Her friend tugged at the bottom of her sweater in an effort to ease the wrinkles on the front. "It's not like any of us brought our coats. Fifty degrees doesn't sound that cold."

"Right, until you realize the sun's not out and the wind is blowing." She pressed her lips together and puckered at her reflection.

Jess gave her a knowing glance. "Gotta look good for Charlie."

"It's not only Charlie. Come on. Many people will be there. I simply want to look my best."

Amused, the other girl sat on the edge of the pull-out bed. "Yeah, right. You've put more makeup on than usual. If I didn't know any better, I'd say you were going to Prom or something."

Alexis scowled at her. "That's stupid. I'm not in a gown and my hair isn't up. I'm only putting in a little effort. Excuse me for trying to look good."

"So Charlie's not swimming?"

"I don't know anyone who is swimming." She screwed the brush of her lip gloss into its bottle and tightened the cap. "It seems like such a weird thing to set up as an activity for a group of high schoolers who barely know each other."

"I guess some people aren't so self-conscious." Jess punched her shoulder playfully.

"Who, me?"

"You know I'm talking about you. You wouldn't be caught dead in a swimsuit around Charlie."

She double-checked her makeup in the mirror, then closed it and tucked it into her duffel bag. "Okay, yeah. I won't wear a swimsuit around him until I have to. Once he comes over to hang out this summer…maybe then. But I'll have more control over my environment there. Plus, I don't know what some of these other girls look like. What if they're knockouts in swimsuits? He'd forget all about me."

"I think you're overreacting."

"High school boys, Jess. Only one thing catches their eye."

"You're right, but Charlie seems like a decent dude. And you look great in a swimsuit. And this conversation is irrelevant anyway. You're dancing, not swimming."

Alexis zipped her duffel bag and sighed. "I hope he doesn't change his mind."

"What, and suddenly decide he wants to go swimming?"

Jess shook her head skeptically. "You're overthinking this. Go and enjoy yourself. He said he won't swim, so he won't. Dance the night away and pretend it's Festival again. You had fun then."

"Yeah, but that was different." She stood and walked to her shoes, which were tucked under a desk chair on the far side of the basement rec room. "There was no pressure there. If it went well, great, if it didn't, fine. I didn't think I had a chance with him anyway, so I was fine simply going out there and having fun."

"So what changed?"

"We did." She sat at the desk to slip her shoes on. "We went from two people who were near each other to possibly dating. He didn't kiss me on the dance floor, though, so now there's all this pressure."

Jess smirked. "Come on. There's no pressure. If things went well because you were being yourself, why wouldn't you… I don't know, keep being yourself? It worked before."

"It's easy for you to say. You don't care about boys."

Her friend put her hands on her hips and scowled at her. "Hey, it's not that I don't care about boys. I want to date boys, too. At the same time, I understand that at this age, boys come and go. If I have a date and lose him, oh well. There are others. But you…"

Alexis closed her eyes, annoyed. "I live and die by the boy who gives me attention. Yes, I know. I create so much pressure with this. But it's how I am. And I bet there are many more girls like me than you."

"At this age, you're probably right, but that's not much of an argument."

Jamie hopped down a few steps and leaned forward to

poke her head past the edge of the ceiling and peer down from the basement stairs. "Hey, what's all the arguing about?"

"We're not arguing." Jess shook her head while she returned to the steps.

"Well, let's go. Mrs. Bader says we'll take a bus from the school. We have to get there on time." She disappeared again.

Jess paused before she ascended and looked at Alexis, who brushed her sweater with her hands. "Hey."

"What?"

"You look great. Charlie won't see any other girls while you're there."

She smiled. "Thanks."

Mrs. Bader dropped the girls off at the school. The air was downright frigid. When they climbed out of the car, Alexis grasped the edges of her cardigan and pulled it tightly around her chest and neck. "Brrrrr!"

Jess shoved her hands in her pockets. "This is stupid. It's such Wisconsin weather."

To Alexis's delight, Charlie was nearby and joked around with a couple of other boys from a high school in Arizona. When he saw her, he excused himself and walked over. "It's cold, hey?"

"How are you in a t-shirt right now?" She shivered.

"I didn't bring a coat but it's okay. I like the cold weather and I'd rather be cold than sweaty. Besides, with all the dancing we'll do, I thought short sleeves would be a wise move."

He smiled at her and suddenly, she felt a different kind of warmth. Although she still shivered with the outside cold, she was now excited. *He talked about all the dancing we'll do. He used the word we. This will be a great night.*

Once the big yellow school buses pulled up in front of the school, a teacher instructed everyone to board but to pause to be counted on the way in. Charlie followed her on one of the buses, and they found a seat near the back as other students piled in.

"I guess they're not keeping to the no boy-girl seating rule for tonight." He smiled at her.

"Good. It's refreshing." *Don't be too eager. Play it cool or he will think you're weird.*

They talked for the entire ten-minute drive to the YMCA, mostly about school and choir. When they arrived at their destination, she was almost bursting with excitement, ready to dance with the cute boy who obviously wanted to spend time with her.

After everyone disembarked, several staff members of the YMCA stepped in to show those students interested in swimming where the locker rooms were and the entrance to the pool. The others were directed to a basketball gym for dancing.

While they walked through the YMCA, Alexis and Charlie passed a large row of windows overlooking the pool area. They stopped to look down and see the setup.

"It looks like a nice pool." He nodded with wry approval. "Too bad I didn't pack a suit."

"Yeah, too bad." She tried to sound sincere although she was relieved that it wouldn't be an issue that evening. "It does look like fun down there. But what's that?"

She pointed to a pair of long brown beams that floated in the water. Two staff members of the YMCA stood in the water on either side of these and rested their arms on them while they joked and chatted.

"Oh, that's for log rolling." He chuckled.

"What's that?"

"It's a thing that people used to do back in the day—lumberjacks or whatever. Those are supposed to be logs, but they're probably plastic. I've done it before. They're hard but, like, kinda soft so you don't break a leg when you bounce off 'em."

Alexis still didn't understand what he meant. "Why would you bounce off one? What do you do?"

"You compete with someone to see how long you can stand on one. That's why there are two of them. They'll let go of the logs while you stand, and the log will spin in the water. You have to see how long you can stay standing before you fall off."

"That actually does sound like fun."

"Yeah, I did it when I was camping with my family one year." They continued their walk down the hall and followed the majority of students who headed to the basketball court. "It's fun because you look like a total goofball when you're up there, flailing your arms and trying to stay on top. It's silly, but it's fun."

Okay, good, then. I would probably embarrass myself on one of those things.

They reached the basketball court, which was set up like a lower-level Homecoming Dance. There were no balloons, no streamers, and no decorations. Stretched along the far wall, up against those bleachers that were not set up, was a row of tables with plates of cookies and juice dispensers. A DJ stood on the other end and blasted "Let's

Get It Started" by The Black-Eyed Peas through the speaker system while his spotlights danced around the room.

The overhead lights were low, and several groups of students were already on the dance floor, obviously enjoying themselves.

Alexis nodded and bounced along with the beat of the music. *This should be fun—a whole group of people who are all into music? A perfect fit for ChoralFest.*

For the next hour, the young couple danced with one another. Their eyes met occasionally and they exchanged nervous laughter. Charlie enjoyed dancing, and his moves were odd and wild. Alexis found it charming and amusing.

They took a break to pour a little punch from a large punch bowl in the center of the row of tables, and he picked up a chocolate chip cookie from a black plastic platter. They shuffled over to a set of bleachers that was set up and sat to rest.

"You have quite the moves." She smiled at him.

He shrugged. "Thanks. I don't really care how I look out there."

"You're not self-conscious about it?"

"Why would I be? You can't spend your whole life worrying about what you look like. We're surrounded by kids we'll probably never see again. I don't care what they think of me."

That is such a healthy attitude. I wish I cared less about how I looked.

CHAPTER TWELVE

W hile Alexis was busy falling even harder for the boy, her father was at home, hoping a woman would fall hard for him.

It sure is cold outside. Craig yanked a black sweater on over a white button-up shirt. He stood in front of the mirror in his room and stared at his outfit. *I wish Alexis was here to give me a little feedback. Do I look too nice for a casual dinner? I'm in jeans, at least. Then again, what do adults wear on a date?*

He pulled the sweater off and opted for only the button-up shirt with his jeans and sighed quietly. His previous dates had not seemed to hold this much pressure.

All those girls from that dating app felt so different. I wasn't nearly as nervous. I didn't care what I wore. Why am I thinking this through so much? Is it because I met this woman outside of those apps?

It had been more than that. Although they had met organically, there was something about Amanda that triggered a wave of feelings in him. While he resisted saying as much, he hadn't met anyone who had affected him like that since Carol had passed away.

While he spritzed a little cologne on the side of his neck, he looked at the clock. "Ooh, I have to go soon," he said out loud to no one in particular.

He had originally tried to set a date up for Friday night, which Amanda agreed to, but she called later and rescheduled to Saturday. She didn't explain why, and he didn't ask. It had worked well as it allowed for Vickie's work schedule as well.

As he walked down the hallway, his brain began to run through all the reasons why she would reschedule at the last minute. *Maybe she had second thoughts. What if she stands me up tonight? What if she decides to go date someone else? Is there someone else? Maybe she has that dating app too, although I've never seen her on it.*

His mind raced on and on, but he snapped out of it long enough to talk to Vickie, who watched a movie in the living room. "You have that giant TV in your room. What are you doing out here?"

She picked the remote up and paused the movie. "Why would I? I have the whole house to myself tonight. I don't want to spend it cooped up in my room."

"Will you be okay on your own? I won't be gone that long." The thought of the vampire alone always gave him pause.

"I'll be fine." She ignored the twisting sensation in her stomach. "I got through my shift last night without using my powers and I should be fine tonight. I'll simply chill out, eat pizza, and watch movies. It'll be nice, actually."

"Okay. How do I look?" He stretched his arms out and displayed his outfit to her.

"It looks good to me. But what do I know?"

He lowered his arms. "Yeah, I know. But Alexis isn't here. I only needed a second opinion."

"Go get 'em." She smiled at him. "I'm sure it'll go great."

"I hope so." He took a deep breath and headed to the door.

The drive to the Olive Garden went quickly but it felt like an eternity to Craig. Exactly as he used to do as a teen when he headed out to dates, he took the opportunity to give himself a little pep talk in the car. He turned the radio off and grasped the steering wheel with both hands while he spoke out loud to himself.

"You've got this, Craig. You know she likes you or she wouldn't be there. And if she isn't there, she isn't the one for you. There are plenty of fish in the sea. You'll simply have fun, be yourself, and relax. Get a scotch when you get there, take the edge off, and enjoy the company. If nothing else, you'll have a good dinner and a beautiful woman to talk to. There are no negatives here."

He pulled into the restaurant parking situated on the opposite end of a lot that included the now-closed Target store and a discount suit store. When he stepped out into the cold night, he shook his head. *This neighborhood really went downhill. I kinda miss walking through that Target.*

He jogged across the lot and stopped to compose himself before he walked through the doors. To his delight —and relief—Amanda had already arrived and waited for him with a smile on her face.

To Craig, she looked incredible. She wore a tight black

sweater with a purple scarf tied loosely around her neck, skinny jeans, and black high-heeled boots. Her hair was pulled back into a ponytail.

"Hey, sorry I'm late."

She raised her wrist and glanced at her watch. "You're not late. I was a few minutes early. I already put our name in, so our table should be ready."

Sure enough, he followed her to the host stand, where they found that they could be seated immediately. They wove through the restaurant, past the obligatory Italian-style decor of murals and fake greenery everywhere they looked, until they reached a small bank of booths.

Once they were seated, he looked around and shook his head. "Man, have I had some bad dates here."

Amanda raised her eyebrows. "Really? You come here a lot?" She picked the menu up and flipped it open.

"Oh, that's not what I meant. I only…I have had some bad dates here." *Jeez, man, way to put your foot in the mouth right out of the gate. Strong start.*

She giggled. "I know what you meant. I'm only teasing you. Now, someone get me breadsticks. I'm hungry."

The woman likes her breadsticks. I'm on board with this. He flagged a server and soon, a piping-hot basket of bread-sticks sat on the edge of their table. "Would you like to dive in?"

She raised her palm. "Actually, as hungry as I am, I'll wait a second. I like to have something to drink while I eat." A minute and a half later, her vodka-cranberry and his scotch on the rocks arrived. "Okay, now I can eat." She rubbed her hands together in excitement and dragged the basket of bread across the table. "This is my favorite part."

Craig watched in amusement as she peeled away the cloth napkin draped around the breadsticks and released a puff of steam into the air. While she watched the steam, he watched her. *That smile. This woman is adorable.*

The two of them feasted on breadsticks and made small talk while they ate. Every few minutes, she would make the same comment. "I really need to slow down and not fill up on breadsticks, or I won't have enough room for when the spaghetti comes." Then, invariably, she'd take another bite.

Sure enough, by the time her plate of spaghetti was on the table, she was full. "I'll eat a little of this but not all of it. I don't think I have space." She giggled at herself as she twisted the fork in the pile of noodles.

He carved into his steak, and the salty crispness of the seared crust made his mouth water. "Oh, this is fantastic. I know Olive Garden isn't exactly the place for a fine steak, but this is really good."

"Is it better or worse than the last steak you had here? You know, on your last date?" She winked at him.

A flurry of nerves hit his stomach. *See? She won't let it go, man. Nice work.*

"I'm only kidding." She burst out laughing. "I had to tease you a little about it, come on. Besides, who am I to talk? We're on our first date and I sit here and guzzle breadsticks like a pig."

Craig laughed with relief. "No, that doesn't bother me. I'm not like that about food. If a woman wants to eat well, great. Order as much as you want." That was the truth, not simply reassurance. He actually found it oddly cute that she was comfortable enough to eat so much in front of him.

She didn't buy it. "Oh, please. It's not exactly ladylike to pound this much food in front of someone else."

He twisted his face in confusion. "Who cares about ladylike? I want you to be yourself. The more, the better. I love food. I'd hate to hang out with someone who constantly counted calories and gave me speeches about the dangers of carbs."

Amanda dabbed the corner of her mouth with her napkin and placed it on her lap again. "Have you had dates like that already?"

"I've had my share of bad dates." He shrugged. "Let's leave it at that. It's hard, dating with kids at home..." Immediately after saying that, he regretted it. *Is that appropriate first-date talk? Will she be so turned off by it that she'll end the date early or something? Shoot. Think these things through, man.*

But again, to his surprise, she wasn't affected by the comment. "I'm with you there. Dating is so much more complicated as a parent. I want whoever I'm dating to be a part of my life, but how do you do that when you have to protect your kid? I don't want my son to get attached to a guy because I go out on a few dates with him. It becomes this weird little dance."

He nodded and folded his hands on the table. "I suppose it helps if you date someone who already knows the struggles you're talking about."

She smiled at him. He marveled at how the small overhead light cast a beam on her face and she almost glowed. The look in her eye was amused but also contained a trace of agreement. It made his heart skip a beat.

"Yeah, it does. I love that I don't have to explain that side of my life. It scares guys off."

"Stupid guys." He stabbed another piece of steak on his plate. "I guess it helps that my girls are older. They know what's going on. One of them told me to go get 'em tonight before I left."

They shared a laugh.

As the night wore on, Craig fell deeper and deeper. He was infatuated with this beautiful woman. They had so much in common, and there was never a dull moment in the conversation. They got along beautifully and he couldn't believe his good fortune.

After they finished eating a few mouthfuls of dessert, Amanda leaned back in the booth. "I don't think I could eat another bite if I tried. This was fun, Craig. It really was."

"I agree. We'll have to do it again sometime."

"Definitely."

After Craig paid the server, the two of them walked out. When they reached the front door leading to the parking lot, he felt overwhelmed with the nerves of a high schooler.

Should I kiss her? What is the standard protocol on a good first date? I can't believe how awkward this all is. No wonder I was so relieved to be married all those years.

Once they approached her car, they exchanged good-byes. Amanda leaned in, gave him a kiss on the cheek, and smiled warmly at him. "Call me, okay?"

"I will."

She drove away and he practically skipped his way to the car. *I haven't had a good first date in ages. And this was a good one.*

CHAPTER THIRTEEN

For Vickie, however, the evening did not go anywhere nearly as smoothly.

After Craig left for his date, she put her feet up and enjoyed a bowl of popcorn while she watched a movie called *Rookie of the Year*, a story about a young boy who broke his arm. When it finished healing and the doctor removed the cast, he learned that he had the throwing ability of a Major League Baseball pitcher. Sure enough, the Chicago Cubs signed him to be a new pitcher for them, and he struck batters out with ninety-miles-an-hour fastballs.

Although it was a lighthearted kids' fantasy from the early nineties, she was befuddled by how it unfolded.

I don't see how breaking his arm would give him the ability to throw baseballs any faster. And is it standard practice for professional baseball teams to hire children to pitch for them? I've seen a few baseball games now and I can't imagine any team with a child on it.

The logistics of the movie aside, her instincts still bothered her. This distracted her from the movie far more than the inconsistencies of its premise.

Her stomach bounced from pained to twisted to an almost upside-down feeling. None of it was comfortable and none of it boded well for her. She did her best to ignore it, but it returned every time she tried to push it aside.

As she watched Henry Rowangardner—the main character in the movie—look up at the camera and flash a World Series championship ring on a freeze-frame to end the film, she shook her head and turned the TV off.

"That was ridiculous." Sometimes, she enjoyed the freedom of being alone in the house. Speaking freely was one of the advantages. "That would never happen in real life." She walked into the kitchen and stared out the window into the darkness of the field behind the house. "Now, what is going on out there? Is someone hanging out in the field and has somehow triggered my instincts? Why am I so uncomfortable? And why can't I simply enjoy a lazy Saturday evening by myself?"

With no clear answers to those questions, she sighed out loud, took another Pepsi out of the fridge, and went to her room to retrieve her laptop. "I am not hanging out in here all night, though. I'll watch something on the TV in the living room. Otherwise, the silence will be deafening."

After she returned to the living room with her laptop in hand, Vickie turned on an old sitcom about a young man from Philadelphia who moved to the west coast and lived with his aunt and uncle. It was another premise that forced her into a state of confusion.

She waved the remote control around as she talked.

"Now, this. Is he a real prince? Why do they call him that? And what makes a prince fresh? Those two words don't go together. He doesn't seem like a prince. He acts like a jester or a clown."

Fortunately for her sanity, she knew that she wouldn't actually watch the show. It was only on to keep the silence from bogging her down too much. Instead, she intended to surf a little on her laptop and hope she could find some answers that would soothe her nerves a little.

While her computer booted up, she stared at the little spinning icon in the middle of the screen. "What am I even looking for? It's not like I can Google *group of guys out in a field in Milwaukee* and I'll get a result. Where do I start?"

Remembering her past online activity, she logged into Reddit and opened the group for real-life vampires. It had been months since she accessed that group as she preferred to focus on her real-life friendships instead. Besides that, ever since her encounter with the Circle, she felt it best if she tried to detach from her life as a vampire.

To her surprise, the front page of the group was peppered with comments and analysis from dozens of the group's members, all focused on the security footage of her destroying the car.

She folded her arms on her chest. *On the one hand, I sure am tired of seeing anything related to this stupid video. On the other hand, I'm curious to see what members of a community that believes in vampires would actually think of something like this. I'm surprised I haven't tried to look on here before.*

Vickie clicked around on the site and read various comments. A few of them impressed her. Many viewed the video as proof that there were vampires in the present-day world. They felt the footage was enough that anyone could see it and believe it themselves. In short, they believed the video was almost divine in nature and justified their belief system.

On the other end of the spectrum, a small handful of commenters and posters believed the footage was doctored as part of some far-reaching conspiracy. A few relegated the video to a marketing stunt that would reveal itself over time. One person on Reddit claimed that it had to be a part of a movie marketing campaign and that some kind of new superhero movie was expected to be released soon that would tie into it.

The rebuttals to many of the conspiracy theories of the video being faked revolved around a screenshot of the video at the forty-five-second timestamp, where a rip in the shoulder of her sweatshirt could be seen. Many of the posters felt that this rip suggested it was not doctored, as no one would bother with that much detail to fake such a sensational video.

The vampire laughed and shook her head at some of these very humorous suggestions. If nothing else, they provided a little distraction and lightheartedness that she hadn't felt for weeks, ever since the incident took place.

Part of her missed browsing around on the forums, as her memories of doing so were some of her earliest in the year that she had been in the present day. She recognized the names of a few posters and she was happy that she was able to read their messages again.

The conspiracy theories, to her, were the most amusing. Some believed she wasn't a vampire and was, in fact, an alien species from a distant planet. That one actually made her chuckle out loud.

Others believed that it was a political stunt, with one message detailing the theory:

What is happening is the government is planning to release legislation that would further damage the American middle class. Any time this happens in history, they release documents, images, videos, and other news that would distract the public from their actions—allowing them to get away with it scot-free. Basically, every major war or scandal in our country's history has been set up by the deep state to ensure that their betrayals are covered up. What will you cover on the news so people will watch—a new tax law or a video of a young girl demolishing a car? Think about it. How has no one seen this girl?

While she chuckled at this one as well, it also confused her. *Is this true? I know nothing about politics. I've been warned to stay away from it.* She was tempted to scratch beneath the surface and start going down that path, but she remembered Craig's stern warning to her a couple of months after they arrived in America.

"At this point, everyone wants to make every conversation about politics. Remember this—almost nothing is political. Worry about taking care of yourself and the people you love. That's it, okay? Don't get caught up in the weeds of politics or it will ruin your life and accomplish nothing."

That day, she'd promised him she wouldn't. So, despite her curiosity, she avoided the conversation about politics and her video.

In the middle of all this, a small notification popped up

on her monitor. It was from Eric, who she hadn't spoken to much in recent weeks.

She was delighted to hear from him. Between all her activities and the general end of the school year hectic schedule, they hadn't connected very much. She looked forward to having a break over summer so they could return to their usual routines.

Eric: *Hey*

Vickie: *Hey! How are you - I haven't been able to talk to you much lately. How is that Physics project going?*

E: *It's going fine, thanks. Not ready for Mr. Festerling to look at yet, but it's coming along, haha*

V: *That's good*

V: *I miss you*

E: *I miss you too. It's weird not getting to really see or talk to each other outside of school hours*

V: *I know. But my uncle says I have to work, you know?*

E: *I know*

E: *Hey*

V: *What?*

E: *We need to talk*

Vickie's heart jumped. She didn't know much about the present day but she understood that "we need to talk" was a huge warning sign for a dating couple.

V: *Is something wrong?*

E: *I don't want to talk about it here*

V: *I know, I'm a little worried, that's all*

V: *Reassure me*

E: *Of what?*

V: *Are you breaking up with me?*

E: *No*

E: *I simply have some questions*

She was relieved to hear that he wasn't thinking of breaking up with her. But this hardly settled her. They agreed to meet earlier than usual at school on Monday morning. He would get a ride so that he could get there a touch earlier and they would have a little time alone.

The rest of the conversation was awkward at best. She was terrified of whatever he wanted to talk about. Two days would be a long time for her to sit and think about it.

The rest of the weekend was a blur. Alexis came home on Sunday evening, flying high off her experience at ChoralFest.

She regaled Vickie with stories of dancing with Charlie and how magnificent the combined choirs sounded together. But the vampire was not visibly excited about any of it.

"What's wrong?" her sister asked.

"I don't know. Eric says he wants to talk tomorrow morning but he won't tell me what it's about."

"Uh oh." The girl sat on the edge of the bed. "Are you worried he'll break up with you?"

"I have no idea. He said he wasn't. But what would he want to talk about?" She paused. "You know, all weekend, my instincts have gone crazy. I don't know what it is. But now, I wonder if this is why. Maybe my powers know something about Eric that I don't."

"I wouldn't sweat it too much. He's not a liar. If he says he's not breaking up with you, he's not."

After a restless night of sleep, she met Eric at the school and opted for a secluded corner near the Band Hall where foot traffic was minimal.

He leaned up against the lockers and looked visibly nervous but tried to seem calm. She greeted him with a kiss.

"I saw something I wanted to talk to you about." The tone in his voice was deadly serious. "I don't know what it is, and I'm not accusing you of anything. I only… Here." He pulled his phone out and held it up to her while he played the video of her incident with the car.

Anger burned inside her. *I can't escape this video. For crying out loud. I had no idea that saving a cute puppy from being run over would ruin my life like this. Wait…what is he saying?* She shifted her attention to him quickly.

"This girl sure looks a lot like you."

Vickie tried to muster a fake smile. "You can't be serious."

"I know, it sounds ridiculous. But look at this. That's you. This is a girl from Clear Lake who runs on the cross country team, and it looks exactly like you. You're even wearing the same shirt right now."

Hastily, she looked at her pink sweatshirt and realized it was a bad day to wear it. *Okay, it's time to act.* "Eric, it could be anyone. You can't see the girl's face. And I would tell you if it was me, wouldn't I?"

"Would you?" He raised his eyebrows, apparently skeptical of her response.

Even though she was lying to him, she couldn't help but

feel a little offended by the reaction. "Hey, I'm not in the business of lying to anyone. Really. Especially you. I want you to trust me. This girl in the video is not me. I don't know who she is. I don't recognize her either. Maybe someone borrowed a Clear Lake shirt. I can't explain it. But I can tell you that it wasn't me. Okay? Can you accept that?"

Although he was frustrated and he still had a feeling it was her, he couldn't argue now that she'd flat-out denied it. "Okay. I trust you. If you say it's not you in the video, it's not you in the video."

The vampire took him by the hand and squeezed it. "Thank you."

She took a few steps and led him along down the hall. He looked at her left shoulder blade where a sizable rip was very noticeable in the fabric of her sweatshirt.

CHAPTER FOURTEEN

On the other side of the school, Jim Trembo marched through the front doors of the building and to the receptionist's window.

The woman at the desk looked at him, adjusted her glasses, and smiled at the handsome stranger in front of her. "Well, hello there. How can I help you today?"

He sensed the energy coming from the woman, leaned forward, and rested his elbow on the counter. "Hi. What's your name?" *Flirt a little, get her guard down, and you're in.*

"Oh, I'm Dana. Dana Filter." She placed her hand on her chest. "I'm the receptionist here at Clear Lake High School."

"Ah, so you practically run the place." He smiled at her.

She uttered a borderline obnoxious laugh. "I wouldn't say that. But anyone who walks through those doors has to get through me first."

"I don't doubt it. Listen, I hoped I could have a few minutes to speak to Mr Goede, your principal here. Is he available?"

Dana tapped on her keyboard. "Let's see…it says he's in his office right now. I think he just got in. I'll message him and see if he would be willing to take an appointment. And your name?"

"James Trembo. I actually work for the federal government."

Her smile dropped. "Oh. Is something wrong?"

He tilted his head and squinted his eyes. "As badly as I want to tell you, I can't divulge that information. All I can do is speak to Mr Goede about it."

"Oh, of course. Give me a minute to check with him. I'm sorry about that."

"No problem, sweetheart." Jim straightened and looked out over the bustling traffic of high school students preparing for the day. *Any one of these kids could be our girl. Imagine that, Jim. After all these years, you're in the same building as one of them. Your entire professional career is within the walls of this high school, breathing the same air you breathe, seeing the same things you see…*

"Mr Trembo?" Dana called out from behind the window. "Mr Goede does have a few minutes to meet with you. Head on down the hall and you'll see his name on the door."

After thanking her, he made his way through the sea of students—some of them directed concerned and irritated looks to the outsider—until he found himself seated in a soft blue chair in front of a desk that read *NED GOEDE, PRINCIPAL* on a placard at the front.

He sat there and ran through his pitch over and over in his head, although Mr Goede was nowhere to be found.

Why was I told I could come in and meet with the guy if he's not even here?

Ten minutes passed and finally, the office door swung open. The short, stocky man with a thin mustache over his upper lip stepped in and inclined his head apologetically. "I am so sorry about that, sir." He extended his hand. "Ned Goede."

"James Trembo. A pleasure to meet you."

With a huff, the principal walked around his desk and sat to face his visitor. "I apologize for the delay. I took a group of students out of town to Onalaska this weekend. Now that I'm back in town, all the work that piled up for me while I was gone is waiting for me. You know how that goes."

Jim chuckled. "Of course. I imagine it's even more difficult for an educator."

"It can be, yes. So, what can I do for you? Dana says you are an official of some kind?"

"That's right." He withdrew his wallet from his pocket and flipped it open to reveal his government-issued ID. "I'm a federal agent on a special investigation, and I was tasked to come here to Clear Lake High School."

Mr Goede furrowed his brow. "You know, I am happy to work with the federal government on whatever they need to investigate. Our school is an open book, and all the practices we engage in here are above reproach."

He laughed and waved airily. "We're not here to investigate you or the school itself, Mr Goede. I appreciate your defense of your school."

"But what are we talking about here? How could we not

get a phone call first? I didn't receive any advance notice that you would be here."

"That's not exactly how we work at times." Jim rested his ankle across his knee. "In situations like these, we play things close to the vest. Very few people know in advance what we are doing."

The man lifted a cup of coffee to his lips and took a sip. "All right, then. What are we talking about here?"

"We have been informed repeatedly in the last several years that doping has become more prevalent in high school athletes."

"Doping?" Mr Goede set his coffee down. "Excuse me? You're talking about steroid use?"

Jim nodded and tried his best to sound convincing. "Yes, but not only steroids. There are growth hormones and other supplements that can give an athlete an unfair advantage over others. Do you implement a drug testing protocol here at Clear Lake, sir?"

The thought made the other man laugh. "Mr Trembo, these are high school kids. No, I don't test them for drugs on a regular basis. There may be drug testing that is done if there is a suspicion of some kind. But that's about it. We aren't looking for hormone drugs or steroids."

"I understand, sir. Well, that's why I'm here."

The principal folded his arms and looked skeptically down his nose at him. "You're here to drug test my students?"

"No, no." *Stay the course, Jim. Be charming.* "What we are trying to determine is whether or not drug testing would be necessary. That's our concern. We don't know if there is enough widespread usage to warrant a national drug-testing program. The government has dispatched a number of representatives to investigate schools of all sizes." *Of course, that number is only one, but don't ask me and I won't have to lie about that part.*

"This is so strange." Mr Goede shook his head. "Investigating high schools for kids on the juice."

"This may be strange, but you'd be shocked at how many things we have to investigate which are so much dumber or more far-fetched than this one. This assignment is fairly tame by comparison."

"I can only imagine." The principal found a notebook and a pen and began taking notes. "What kind of access do you need? How can we make this as efficient as possible for you and for the school? Frankly, our students won't tolerate having someone randomly watching them on a long-term basis. School will be over soon anyway, so it will be important to have this wrapped up in a timely fashion."

"Of course. I can respect that." Jim paused to think for a moment. *This is working. Give him the right answers to these questions and you're in.* "Obviously, I'd need a schedule of upcoming athletic events for the rest of the school year. I'd like to attend and experience those for myself."

"That's no problem at all." Mr Goede continued to scribble notes. "And you're welcome to meet with any of the faculty members as you wish. I can arrange those meetings."

Another step. Good. "Most of my investigations will be freeform, let's say. I'd need to be able to move around the school and see these kids in their natural environment." He winked at the principal and laughed. "I don't mean to make them sound like lab rats. I simply want to be able to watch them interact on a day-to-day basis without my intrusion. Instead of sitting them down and interviewing them all individually, it would be more effective if I move among them."

The man leaned back in his chair and tapped the edge of his pen to his chin. "I know what you're saying. I'll have to think about that, though. I don't want to get in the way of the federal government, but you understand that I can't give you a green light to walk through the school, either. There have to be some parameters for the sake of our students' privacy."

Find a way, Jim. "Okay, I don't need to see them during classes or in any…shall we say, private moments. I would need to see them at sporting events, like we've discussed, and in the halls, maybe at lunchtime. Stuff like that—places where they interact publicly."

He waited while the other man clearly wracked his brain to come up with a solution. "How about this? We create a special role for you as a hall monitor of sorts. That way, we can establish to the students why you are there, no one will want to get in your way, and I can also message the parents and explain your presence as well."

"I like it." He nodded. *You're almost there.* "The last thing, then, would be access to the students' contact information. Surely you have a database of some kind?"

"I do, yes." He had clear hesitation in his voice. "But that is for school use only. The federal government would have its own database—"

"Right, but we're looking to make this efficient. You can imagine that the federal government is hardly an efficient operation." They both laughed. "I don't want to intrude on privacy. But if we do discover anyone who might be…um, enhancing themselves, we would need direct access to them."

"I'll tell you what. I can facilitate that. We can organize meetings here in the school. That way, everything is in-house and I don't have to release records to a third party." He stood from his desk and looked out the window at the traffic that moved past the school. "Here's the thing, Mr. Trembo. I have never done anything like this before. I don't exactly know how to handle it. While I want to make sure I assist you in the best way possible, at the same time, I can't betray the trust and confidence that the students and their families have placed in me and my faculty by attending this school."

Jim stood and shook his hand. "I understand completely, and I appreciate you working with me on this. I'll make sure you and your faculty are protected. If we do need contact information, I'll provide you with a warrant to legally protect you."

The thought of a warrant being issued for one of his students made the principal shift in his shoes but he could not fight the plan. He knew it was the right thing to do and he would do it.

As his visitor walked out of the office, the principal began to draft an email to the faculty discussing the details of the meeting.

CHAPTER FIFTEEN

Vickie slammed her locker door after changing into a pair of khaki shorts and a black t-shirt. After a quick glance at her pink cross country sweatshirt, she shook her head, stuffed it into her backpack, and zipped it.

What a day. My presentation group from phys-ed can't decide how to work together. I had to talk my way out of getting caught by Eric. And I can't seem to shake the queasy feeling that something bad is happening. I want to go home and curl up in bed for the rest of the night.

"Are you all right?" Krista walked over to her as she slung her backpack over her shoulders.

"I'm fine." She sat on the bench to tie her shoes. "It's only one of those days."

Her friend nodded. "Yeah. I've been there." She looked at her watch. "Hey, we have time before our rides get here to pick us up. Let's go shopping. I'll buy you chocolate. No bad day can't be helped with a little chocolate."

She straightened on the bench and looked at the girl,

who was earnestly trying to help. "Okay. Let's go get chocolate."

Very often, track and cross country practices continued beyond the expected finish times. It wasn't uncommon for drivers to sit in their cars for fifteen or twenty minutes while they waited for the runners to come out.

That day, however, Coach Lueck kept the workout light and the run short, and everyone had almost half an hour to kill before their rides arrived. Some students texted their parents. Others with licenses simply hopped in their cars to drive home.

A few, including Krista and Vickie, took the unexpected time as an opportunity to chill, hang out, and decompress after a long day.

They stepped out of the back exit of the school building and turned left to walk up the ramp leading to the sidewalk.

"How are you feeling heading into this weekend's meet?" Krista loved talking about running more than anything else.

"I feel fine. My legs were a little tight today, but they'll loosen up by Saturday." Vickie's legs were not tight at all. But this deep into her running career, she had made note of the different kinds of aches and pains runners typically complained about. To her, having the option of complaining about a common injury was a great way to sound like a realistic teenager.

"Man, my ankle has nagged me lately. I don't know if it'll totally hobble me this weekend if it doesn't clear up, but it'll probably affect me. I might have to grit my teeth and run through the pain."

They rounded the corner and walked into the parking lot of the grocery store as Vickie made another mental note. *My ankle has nagged me lately and might hobble me, whatever that means.*

While they traversed the lot, she looked over her shoulder at Bluemound Road. A little west of where they were was the site of the accident that exposed her powers to the general public. Every time she found herself near Bluemound Road, it crossed her mind—which happened often since Clear Lake High School was one block away from there.

As it usually did, her stomach began to tighten as she thought about it. *Another reminder. I get it. You can calm down, instincts. I know I screwed up there and I'm not out of the woods yet.*

"How are you and Eric doing?"

The vampire shrugged. "Fine, I guess. Nothing new there." *Except for one big, obvious new thing but hopefully, that will pass.* "We haven't had all that much time to hang out lately." *Okay, body, I get it. I'm near Bluemound. Calm down. Jeez.*

"Summer will be here soon. If you're going to be around for it, I'm sure you'll be able to hang out then. Will you get your license this year?"

"I haven't really discussed it with anyone yet. I guess I could." *Come on, stomach, give me a break.*

Her entire body tensed and she didn't know why. This was more extreme than she had felt all day, and much tighter and more painful than she had ever felt while reliving her mistake on Bluemound Road.

Near the entrance to the store, two workers stood on

opposite ends of a thick wooden scaffold stretched across two adjustable legs on wheels. The temporary platform raised them to the height of the large, red Pick 'n Save sign that hung above the automatic doors.

"I wonder what they're doing. Is that a new sign?" Krista wondered aloud and frowned at the remaining Pick 'n S that was still up.

Vickie stopped walking when she heard a faint but distinctive ping. She stared at the scaffolding with rapt attention, her eyebrows pulled together. As she watched, the ends of the scaffold squeaked and creaked against the metal legs and trembled with each step that the workers took.

Krista was several feet in front of her before she realized that her friend was no longer at her side. "Hey, are you coming or what?"

"Hang on." The vampire didn't make eye contact with her and continued to stare at the scaffold. *You can't use your powers. Don't use your powers. Whatever you do.*

Without tapping into her super-speed, she sprinted toward the scaffold and moved as fast as humanly possible.

"Hey!" The other girl held out her hands, palms up. "What are you doing?"

She ignored her and continued to run, pushing herself to go as fast as she could. *Come on. I can't use my powers but I need to get there in time. I can do this.*

When she was within ten yards of the scaffolding, a snapping sound rang out across the parking lot. In the same moment, an old woman wearing bright red lipstick and a thick, brown fur coat sauntered out of the store and was about to step under the temporary framework.

That's it. Go, go go!

Once she was close enough, Vickie leapt forward to tackle the old woman, who shrieked in alarm. Thinking ahead, she spun herself as she came down and rolled so the frailer body could fall on top of her and be somewhat protected.

They had no sooner landed when the left edge of the scaffolding fell as the leg that supported it collapsed. The worker on that side fell awkwardly to the pavement, and the other man slipped and rode the platform like a slide before he landed hard on his coworker. The entire contraption tumbled.

Onlookers were stunned. Krista stood with her mouth agape and stared at Vickie while she tried to process her friend's heroic action.

Still on the ground, the vampire uttered a quiet moan.

"Are you all right, dear?" The old woman spoke in a sing-song voice. "That was quite a fall you took."

Her vision blurred, she blinked and shook her head. The multicolored shapes she could see eventually transformed into the lady who knelt beside her. "Are you okay?" She could barely gasp the words and struggled to drag in a breath.

"Oh, I'm fine, sweetheart." She clutched her small black leather purse. "You took the worst of it."

Vickie couldn't deny that. Every time she inhaled, she felt as though she was drowning. *Something isn't right. I can't breathe.* Her face turned a deep shade of red as Krista ran up.

"Vickie—oh, my gosh, are you okay?" She dropped to

her knees beside her. "You are turning all kinds of colors. You look blue. We need to call an ambulance."

An ambulance? If doctors get their hands on me, they might discover I'm not human. There's no way I can let an ambulance come.

Krista pulled her cell phone out, but she swatted it away with the little strength she had.

"Hey! I'm trying to help. We need to get you to the emergency room."

She rested her head on the pavement and rolled it from side to side. "Get me into the store and into the bathroom."

"You can't be serious." Her friend's mouth hung open in disbelief. "You need a doctor."

"She's right, honey." The old woman nodded. "A doctor can make sure you're okay."

Her teeth gritted, she widened her eyes and gave the girl a very serious glare. "Please, get me to the bathroom."

Shaking her head, Krista helped her begrudgingly to her feet and dragged one of her arms over her shoulders. The vampire winced in pain, doubled over, and clutched her abdomen. After a moment, she straightened and managed a shaky smile she hoped would reassure her companion.

While the workers who fell off the scaffolding attempted to clean the shattered glass and inspected themselves for injury, she limped slowly into the store against the protests of the old woman.

Eventually, the elderly lady thanked her and walked away, obviously feeling that she could do no more to help. Krista moved forward and almost dragged her friend through the store amidst stares from onlookers.

"This is ridiculous. You need to see someone." The girl pushed the bathroom door open. "What do you want in here?"

"Get me to a stall. The wide one down there." She nodded her head at the handicapped stall at the far end of the bathroom.

Once they were there, Krista took a deep breath. "Now what? Do you need help in here, or what?"

Vickie sat on the toilet seat and looked at her. "I only need privacy now. Wait outside."

All but speechless, her companion could only stutter various syllables in confusion.

The vampire remained adamant. "I only need a minute. Please."

The other girl stormed out of the bathroom and Vickie waited for the sound of the door closing. Tears streamed down her cheeks as she struggled to push through the pain. Hunched over with her arms wrapped around her stomach, she attempted to take a few deep breaths.

While she didn't feel as though she was breathing deeply enough, she was able to concentrate hard and the energy began to flow through her veins. After a few moments, her ribs mended themselves and moved back into place accompanied by an odd sensation of warmth and a couple of odd snaps.

With the pressure finally off her lungs, she gasped loudly, leaned to her left, and rested the side of her face against the cold tile wall. *Holy cow, that hurt.*

She rose to her feet and stretched her back, satisfied that she definitely felt better. To keep up the charade, she kicked the handle of the toilet to flush it and walked over to the sink to wash her hands.

While she scrubbed her palms, she stared in the mirror, relieved that the color had dissipated from her face. *At least it was me and not the old lady. She could have been killed. That would have been ugly. This is so much easier when I can use my powers. I hate being handicapped like that.*

She turned the water off and snatched a paper towel. *I don't know if I can do things like this if I don't have my powers at my disposal. I'm happy this one worked out, but that was really close. I only want to help people. Is that so bad?*

To Krista's astonishment, Vickie strolled out of the bathroom looking like normal. "How is that possible? You looked like you were going to keel over."

"I told you." She shrugged. "I only needed a few minutes."

"How did you know that the scaffold was going to fall?"

"Um…I heard the screw pop. It looked shaky. I had a feeling, I guess."

The two of them suddenly had no appetite for chocolate, so they headed out the door to the parking lot, where the workers still attempted to repair the equipment.

CHAPTER SIXTEEN

Whew, that was close. Vickie slipped into the library a second before the bell rang in the hallway. She paused to absorb the usual atmosphere that always appealed to her—the thick silence that hung in the air, the line of librarians checking books in and out, and the pockets of students huddled at tables and in lounge chairs reading books.

I miss this place. She cracked a half-smile. *It's been months since I've been here. This is such a cool atmosphere for studying. And there's why I haven't been coming here.* Her gaze settled on Tricia, who was seated at a table and chatted with a freshman boy.

The vampire didn't recognize the boy but he wore a wrinkled, dirty flannel shirt and khaki shorts that clearly hadn't been washed in a few wears. He was deeply interested in everything Tricia had to say and the girl, having a rapt audience, rambled on.

Out of the corner of her eye, she saw Vickie walk past. She tried to continue talking but was thrown off by the distraction. Their eyes met, and they exchanged polite but cold smiles.

Inside, it hurt her to see Tricia. Her once-friend looked like she hadn't slept in weeks and her clothes were enough on the ragged side to be noticeable. Huge bags hung under her eyes and her skin was pale.

She had to keep walking but all she wanted to do was stop and help her. But how could she?

The girl still didn't believe she needed any help. In contrast to the vampire's inner turmoil, she was fine with the fact that Vickie kept walking. She didn't want to see her anyway. In her mind, she had simply tried to be a good friend to her, a new girl who needed friends.

But even though she had tried to show her a good time in her own way, they hadn't hung out or even really spoke since Tricia had her over to her house. It was for the best.

I wonder what's wrong with her. What is she into now? Did her boyfriend get her hooked on something? I wish I could get her out of that environment, but I don't even know where I would go with her. Vickie shook it off and turned the doorknob on the study room on the outside wall of the library.

Waiting inside were two of the three members of the presentation group she was a part of for phys-ed class. Sam Trissel sat with a blank notebook page open in front of him. Emily Zimmerman spun back and forth in one of the desk chairs surrounding the small meeting table and smiled widely when she walked in.

"Hey, Vickie!"

"Hi, guys." She stepped in, pulled a seat up at the table, and dropped her backpack on the floor beside her. "Where's Adam?"

"He's not here yet." Sam was a polite young man and a little on the quiet side. She wasn't sure how well the four of them would work together but she was more worried about Adam than Sam.

After a few minutes of awkward small talk, the missing group member walked into the study room with a smug smile on his face. "What's up, study group?"

"What took you so long?" She scowled at him.

"Jeez, relax. I had stuff to do, you know?" He plopped into the nearest chair and put his feet on the table.

"You know, if you sign in late, you get a tardy." She honestly had no idea how she was coming across. To her, rules were rules.

Adam scratched one of his sideburns. "Hey, Vic, relax. I get tardies all the time. They can simply add it to the pile of detentions."

"Where's your backpack? Did you bring anything to take notes?" Her patience had worn thin in a matter of minutes.

He leaned back a little more and picked at one of his fingernails, his expression something between amused and scornful. "What's there to note? We'll give a presentation on running, and we have one of the stars of the cross country team here on our squad. This shouldn't take long."

The other two turned to look at Vickie.

"Me? You expect me to do all the work?"

"I wouldn't put it like that." His voice dripped with insincerity. "Look at it like this—the best place to start on these projects is with whatever information you already know, right? You don't reinvent the wheel. Well, we have a runner here so she already knows all the important information about running. I bet you know enough that we could get by on this whole project. It's not like our presentation has to last forty-five minutes or anything."

Sam chuckled at that and smirked eagerly at the other boy as if he waited for some kind of approval from the cool kid. Adam generally avoided eye contact with his classmates in these scenarios and preferred to fidget with his fingernails or stare at various objects in the room.

Currently, a motivational poster that depicted an iceberg protruding from a body of water and the reveal of the gargantuan chunk of ice under the surface had caught his eye, and he stared blankly at it while the others talked.

Emily rolled her eyes at him but agreed with his opinion. "He's right, in a way. You have the most experience with running, which means you could probably lead this project. I don't mind leading it, but I think it would be smarter if you did."

Vickie was ready to put her head down on the table. *I don't want to be here. I have no idea what these kinds of projects entail. I've never spoken in front of people before. And now I'll be stuck giving the presentation?*

"No."

Adam frowned. "What do you mean, no?"

"I mean, no." She adopted a forceful tone of voice. "I won't lead this presentation."

Everyone looked at each other in apparent shock. "Vickie, you're clearly the best person to talk about running." Emily doodled in her notebook as she talked and the way she tapped her foot at the same time indicated a touch of nerves. "It only makes sense. We all want a good grade here, so putting you front-and-center would give us the best chance."

Sam nodded silent agreement with her.

"Too bad. I'm not ready to lead a presentation in front of the entire student body."

Adam dropped his feet to the floor. "Come on. It's not that hard. You simply stand there and talk. What's the big deal?"

"If it's not that big a deal, why don't you do it?" Vickie folded her arms and regarded him with a challenging expression.

His tone of voice suggested he thought it was a stupid question. "Because I'm not a runner. If we were giving a presentation on the health benefits of playing the electric guitar, maybe I would lead it. Shoot, I'd crush that one."

Sam laughed and shook his head at the silly hypothetical situation.

"The best way to run these groups is by pinpointing what everyone's strengths are." Emily wrote each group member's name in her notebook. "I can do considerable research very quickly. Sam, what do you do?"

"Um, I don't know. I'm handy, I guess. If we need a visual aid or something, I could probably put that together."

"Perfect." Emily wrote CONSTRUCTION next to his name. "Adam?"

"What?"

"What's your strength?"

"Delegation." He blew a bubble with the gum in his mouth. It popped and wrapped itself around his nose. He nibbled on it to pull it off his nose and back into his mouth. "I'm great at directing traffic."

"You're unbelievable." Vickie shook her head and rolled her eyes. "This is dumb."

"Okay, and Vickie..." Emily pressed on, obviously hoping to diffuse the situation. "I'd say your strength is knowledge of running. The subject matter is a perfect fit. We simply have to get these pieces to fit together the right way, and we'll get an A for sure."

The problem was, she actually didn't know that much about running. *I am a distance runner, but so much of what I do is only me running fast because I don't get tired. I don't know about the health benefits or how a human being would do it properly. And that doesn't even touch on actually getting in front of the students and doing a presentation on it.*

"Just because I'm a runner doesn't mean I know that much," she admitted. "I simply show up and do what the coach tells me to do."

Adam pursed his lips in frustration. "Great, so now we have a runner who doesn't know anything about running? That's real useful."

"Good one, Adam!" Sam laughed again and drew annoyed looks from the two girls.

Emily rubbed her eyes and drew a few more lines in her notebook. "What do you want to do? What is something that you can do that will help the group and you'll be comfortable with?"

"I don't know." *I can see why Krista hates these group projects. This is driving me insane.*

The girl ran her finger down the worksheet detailing the project. "Oh, it says here that all of us have to make presentations. That means each of us will have to get up in front of the school to talk."

"Great." Adam popped another bubble. "We can each embarrass ourselves individually. That sounds like fun."

"I think it's to ensure that everyone shares the responsibility." She underlined that portion of the directions. "Maybe teachers have caught on to the fact that some students don't do their share of the work." She smiled teasingly at Adam but he didn't acknowledge it.

"Okay, fine." He stood quickly. "I'll go start researching my portion of the presentation."

Anger burned inside Vickie. "But we haven't even started to discuss what we'll talk about."

He shrugged. "Yeah, because we don't know what we're talking about. I'll go start reading up on running and its health benefits so I can decide on my portion of the presentation." With that, he walked out of the room.

Exasperated, Emily looked at the other two and shook her head. "I guess this meeting is over for today."

Vickie sat in utter disbelief. *I will get a bad grade on this project and it's completely out of my control. How am I supposed to make sure he does his job? Okay, let's give him a break. Maybe he will genuinely try his best here and he simply hasn't gotten very far yet. I'm sure the studying he does this period will help him out.*

The group scattered into the library and she chose a small table near one of the windows overlooking the parkway. She sat and jotted notes on what she would want to research and talk about.

After a moment, she looked over at one of the comfortable lounge chairs, where Adam sat with one leg swung over the armrest while he sat sideways in the chair. At one point, he held the book in his hands high enough that she could read the spine.

The A-Z Guide to the Mafia.

She pinched the bridge of her nose. *He's not even doing any research. He's only wasting time. I'm screwed.*

CHAPTER SEVENTEEN

Jim Trembo heard a knock at his hotel room door as he finished the half-Windsor knot in his dark-brown tie. When he opened the door, Pete Stabone stood in front of him.

"Do you have a sec?"

"Sure, Pete, come on in." He closed the door behind them. "It'll have to be quick, though. I don't want to be late for school." He laughed at his own joke. The other man smirked but was clearly not amused. "Are you okay?"

"I'm fine." Pete sat on the edge of the second queen bed in the room. "How long will this take?"

"The school thing?" He turned to face the mirror and ran a comb through his hair. "It all depends. How long did it take us to get the balloon project rolling? How long did it take us to find that area in the field and analyze it? How long—"

The other man raised his hands quickly. "Okay, okay, I get it. I'm only... Jim, I miss my wife and kids. I miss my own bed. Aren't you tired of sleeping in a hotel?"

He nodded sympathetically. "Of course. And I understand what you're saying. I've noticed your enthusiasm for this project has been up and down lately."

"I'm still excited about the project, obviously, but I'm exhausted. I don't sleep well in hotels. What do we still need to do here?"

Jim stuck his arms into a plaid sport coat. "I need a team behind me, Pete. Without you guys, I don't stand a chance. I'll find this girl from the video. When I do, I have to bring her in. That's why you guys need to be there too."

Pete rested his hands on his knees. "Then tell me how long we'll run with this attempt."

"I don't know. I really don't. I know the school year will be over soon. That obviously puts a definite limit on how long I can spend in the school." He turned. "How do I look? Do I look like a hall monitor?"

His companion rolled his eyes and laughed. "As much as anyone could. Don't you need a sash that says *HALL MONITOR* on it?"

"I sure hope they don't give me one."

"I trust you, Jim, and I'm excited by all this too. But I am also ready to go home."

He walked over and slapped him on the shoulder. "Buddy, when I find this girl, we'll walk home with millions of dollars in the bank. This will all be worth it, trust me."

The two men parted ways. When he arrived at the school, Jim first made a few comments to Dana at the front desk and slipped in a little more flirtatious energy in case he needed to cash in on it later. *It never hurts to have a few people on your side. Always think ahead.*

She told him to head back to Mr Goede's office. This time, the principal was there waiting for him. After a quick handshake, he gave him the rundown. "Okay, Jim, the staff and faculty here know you will be patrolling the halls. The best thing you can do is simply make sure you aren't really all that noticeable. That'll obviously be a little difficult since you're taller than virtually all our students, but we'll do our best here. I would suggest that, unless an altercation was in play, you would be wise to avoid any interactions with our students."

He was ready to reassure the man. "I'm not here to make friends or connect with the kids. I only want to watch how they interact with each other, that's all. If you can pinpoint certain telltale activity, you can be fairly certain there is some extra—" He caught himself before he admitted to the real purpose for his visit. "Drug treatments in use."

The principal gestured to the door. "Well, the school is all yours. Please feel free to pop in if you have any questions."

Jim nodded and stepped out into the hallway. He walked to the main area of the lobby and posted himself as guard to keep an eye on everyone as they milled about before their school day began.

He squinted repeatedly and tried to make out the differences between the girls while he hoped he could find one who fit the figure in the video.

The first bell of the day rang and all the kids rushed off to class.

All except one.

From the second Jim Trembo had stepped onto the campus, she was doubled over with pain. Her stomach twisted almost immediately and it took all her energy to release that tension.

Throughout the morning, Vickie returned to the bathroom, chose another large stall, and did whatever she could to calm herself and gain some measure of control over whatever was troubling her.

The feeling came in waves. One moment, she would feel mildly irritated or uncomfortable—anxious but not necessarily in pain. In the next moment, she would feel as though someone had stabbed her in the abdomen.

During the first period of the day, all the students piled into their classrooms. Vickie sat in a bathroom stall, hunched over as she fought to keep herself from grunting audibly in pain.

This is so bad. I can't ignore this any longer. I have to do something. Is this because I can't use my powers? Is there a threat out there somewhere that I haven't addressed? What is it?

Multiple times, she stood in the stall, took a few deep breaths, and placed her hand on the latch of the door. By the time her fingers touched the cold metal, the pain washed over her again and forced her to sit again and try to calm herself through the next onslaught.

Outside, Jim Trembo paced the main lobby of the school and occasionally passed the door of the girls' bathroom.

Okay, Jim, you're in. This is it, baby. Now, what would be the best mode of operation here? Should you pay attention to any particular group? It's not like you can single out the cross country runners in the halls. For one thing, you don't know who they are. Maybe if you asked for a yearbook, you could narrow it down. That might be an option. But today, you're probably better off simply observing what's going on. Watch everyone, take it all in, and get a feel for the crowd here. That's the only way you'll ever really learn about the students. If you see something out of the ordinary, great.

He opted to descend the main stairway and go to the lower lobby in order to familiarize himself with the layout while the school wasn't full of teenagers on the move.

Once he reached the downstairs level, the pain that tortured Vickie disappeared. She made it out of the bathroom stall. A glance in the mirror confirmed that the color had returned to her face. *I won't be able to hide this for long if it keeps up. I need to find the source of it and fast.* She exited the bathroom at virtually the same time that the bell rang for everyone to go to homeroom. She jogged quickly down the hall to let her teacher know she wasn't feeling well, and that was why she hadn't been in class.

Jim Trembo wandered the halls and studied all the students who filed through the corridors on their way to their homerooms. He nodded politely to a few of them. Many of the boys looked at him as though he was some creepy weirdo or stalker. A few of the girls gave him dreamy eyes—something he hadn't considered. *I suppose I'm an older, mysterious man to some of these kids. I'd better be careful who I talk to. The last thing I need is for anyone to get the wrong impression.*

Even though he thought that, talking to the kids was not on his radar at all. He was only there to observe and to collect as much information as he could. His purposes did not include an attempt to make friends or be the cool new guy.

The students reached their homerooms, and he marveled at how cavernous the school building was in between classes. *It's like there's no one here. Amazing. At one point, it's more crowded than a mosh pit, and in the next minute, they're gone.*

As entertained as he was by it, he hadn't really gleaned any information. Although he'd stashed a notebook in his back pocket with a small pen, he had no need to use it to jot anything down. The morning was entirely and disappointingly uneventful.

On the other side of the school, Vickie tried to pay attention to the homeroom announcements with mixed success.

At the front of the room, Brad Johnson read the news of the day and one item was particularly interesting.

Starting this week, a new hall monitor will be in the halls, monitoring students' activity. He will be a temporary member of the staff, and you are expected to show him the same respect you show the rest of the faculty here at Clear Lake High School.

"So, none at all, then?" One class clown obviously couldn't help himself in the back of the room.

They continued with the announcements. Vickie heard the note about the hall monitor but failed to see any significance to it. Rather, she was preoccupied with the intense bursts of pain she had been subjected to, and she wondered when she would have to deal with another one.

The next few hours passed uneventfully. Trembo still struggled to find anything of value. *This place is simply bustling with regular teenagers. There's no supernatural activity here that I can see. I wonder if it's a time of day thing. Maybe the afternoon will be better. But without any of my measuring equipment, there's not much I can do unless someone shows their hand.*

Doubts raged in his brain and bounced disconcertingly into his thoughts while he tried to decide what he should do next.

Normally, he was a patient man. When investigating what he felt was his strongest opportunity to engage with supernatural activity—the fabled Zombie Army project—he had spent months working with his team to analyze the alleged ability to reanimate the deceased.

They studied brains, arms, legs, hearts, and other various organs. Month after month, they tried to instill life into something that no longer lived.

After nearly two years of testing only that aspect of the project, they came away with nothing.

The testing phase didn't bother him. He knew it was part of the deal and he knew that his patience would pay off.

But standing in the lower level of a Milwaukee high school, staring at a softball trophy won in 1984 through the glass of a trophy case, made him very anxious. He wondered how he would ferret out a supposed supernatural being hiding among a student body of more than a thousand kids.

I've never been this close before. Everything has lined up. It's practically been easy at this point. Why can't I seem to get myself through this? It's the first day and I'm ready to give up before lunchtime? Are Pete's concerns this morning getting to me? Since when did I become so impatient?

Despite his reservations, he soldiered on and continued to watch the kids. He saw nothing unusual or out of the ordinary and used the hours during classes to explore every nook and cranny of the school. Through it all, he took care to at least try to not appear to be a random creepy guy who stalked the halls of a high school with no easily explainable reason for his presence.

CHAPTER EIGHTEEN

Craig whistled as he parked his SUV outside Ally's Bistro, a small cafe north of Milwaukee in the suburb of Menomonee Falls.

The parking lot was situated in the middle of several different locations, including an apartment complex, a spa, a bar, and a gym. At the south end stood Ally's Bistro, which offered both indoor and outdoor seating.

He smiled as he stepped out of the vehicle and adjusted his sunglasses. *It looks like the patio is open. I'm not surprised. It's such a beautiful day today.* Indeed, with blue sky overhead and the sun beaming down on him, it was hard to not be in a good mood.

Amanda waited for him at the front door in a spaghetti-strap top and black jeans. She greeted him with a smile. "Hey."

"Will you always be here earlier than me when we get together?" He stepped ahead of her to open the door.

"Well, there's a real simple solution to that."

"I get here at the time I say I'll get here. What's wrong with that?"

"In my book, if you're not early, you're late." She smirked at him.

"I'll try to be better in the future." *She's so playful. I love it. Everything seems so easy and so natural.*

Ally's Bistro was swamped. Neither expected it and they paused for a moment to survey the interior.

"Wow! I guess this is a popular place." Craig scanned the area for an open table. "That's a good sign, though, I guess."

"You've never been here before either?"

"No, it only opened in the past year. I've looked for an excuse to come here, actually. Thanks for being that excuse."

He smiled at her and she returned it awkwardly as she felt he was a little cheesy but thought she should simply run with it.

At this particular cafe, customers stood in line to place their order, then found their own place to sit. While they waited their turn, they huddled around a menu.

"I think I'll simply have the Caesar Salad." She pointed to the listing under the *Sides & Soups* section. "I can even add a little chicken."

"Is that all you'll have?"

She shrugged. "It's lunch. I don't need to eat a huge meal. Besides, at a new place, I like to start with a good salad."

"Why?"

"That's how I know if it's a good place to eat or not. How do you test a place?"

Craig smiled excitedly. "I go for whatever is the first thing on the menu. If it looks like their signature dish, I'm in. I like to start at the thing they pride themselves on. If that's good, I know I have a good place to eat."

"Okay, I can see that logic. What's on the menu that looks like the specialty?" She flipped it and tried to find the main dishes that were highlighted.

He stopped her and pointed to the top of the *Sandwiches* section of the menu. "Here we go. The Number Four—a grilled chicken sandwich with provolone cheese, bacon, crispy onions, and avocado, served on a salted pretzel bun. That might be the most delicious description I've ever read."

They shared a laugh. Once they reached the front of the line, they ordered, Craig paid, and they were handed a placard with the number fifty-four on it. The two of them carried their drink cups to the soda machine to get refreshments and chose to sit outside, away from the loud, bustling activity of the busy dining room.

"My ears are almost ringing." Amanda chose a table in the sun and they both slid their sunglasses back on.

"I'm pumped for this sandwich." He rubbed his hands together. "It sounded delicious. Too bad this place doesn't have cheese curds, though. That would be the ultimate."

"You're a curd man?"

"I'm a big-time curd man. The squeakier, the better. I actually shouldn't talk about it too much or I'll be so in the mood for curds that I won't enjoy my sandwich."

He slipped the number placard into a holder at the edge of the table. By the time he had wiggled it in, a waitress arrived with two plates.

"That was fast!" He raised his eyebrows in shock. "No wonder this place is so busy with service like this!"

She laughed. "We knew you were hungry, so we hurried as quickly as we could. Enjoy the meal."

Amanda took a mouthful of her salad, and he bit into his sandwich. Within seconds, he moaned audibly with delight—and was almost obnoxious with his show of enjoyment.

"Do you want to settle down over there?" she asked and began to feel a little weirded out by the quirkiness of her date. "I'm trying to enjoy my salad."

"This might be the best sandwich I've ever had." He dabbed his mouth with a napkin. "Wow. Something about that pretzel bun really ties the whole thing together. How's the salad?"

"It's great. Really." She swallowed another mouthful. "I'm very impressed. You're right, this place is fantastic."

She's not a food snob and she appreciates a good restaurant. Look at her—even in the middle of the day, she's a knockout.

She caught him staring at her and turned awkwardly away to take another mouthful. He continued to stare for a few more seconds, a half-smile on his face.

The two of them continued to eat and enjoyed every last crumb of their meal. Amanda, in an attempt to move the conversation into other areas, asked him about his car.

"It's doing great. Finally." He laughed. "The guys at your shop do great work. Expensive work, but great work. I was pleased."

"Well, good." She nodded while she scooped up the last of her salad. "I'm happy. It would be really awkward right now if they had done a crappy job."

He laughed again. "Nope, nothing awkward about this date, that's for sure."

Amanda couldn't agree. There was something about the vibe that he gave off that concerned her. A few times during the lunch, she shifted in her chair and tried to shake off the sense of discomfort.

Maybe he's nervous. Or maybe he's not. What if our good date was because he was nervous and this is how he is all the time?

Craig didn't pick up on her concerns. His mind raced with possibilities. *Imagine being able to enjoy this all the time. This is the new normal. She's great. You're great together. It's a perfect fit. Just like that and you weren't even looking for it.*

"It's a heck of a day for a lunch outside." He looked at the blue sky. "People knock Wisconsin for the weather, but when it's on, it's really on."

She smiled politely. "Yeah. This is a really nice day. It makes for a great lunch."

"And hey, we have the whole summer ahead of us. I work from home so I can do this around your schedule. I don't know about you, but I'd like to keep working my way down the menu here."

"Really?" She stopped chewing.

"Yeah, why not? If they have anything else on the menu that's half as good as this sandwich, I think we're in for a real treat. I want to know about it, you know?"

Her smile fell and she inhaled deeply through her nose. "Craig—"

"Weekends could be fun, too. I'm sure the girls would love to get in on this. This could be, like, our place. Wouldn't that be fun?"

Bad sign. You can't let him go on like this. He's too nice a guy to lead on. Amanda put her fork down. "Craig, I don't... I mean...that's really booking things out kinda far, don't you think?"

"Oh, I'm sorry!" He tapped his forehead. "Duh. You probably want to choose places, too. I'm not one of those guys who always has to have the final say in where we eat. I didn't mean to come across that way."

"No, it's not that. We've really only been on one date other than this lunch."

"Sure, but aren't things going well? Aren't you having a good time too?"

She nodded slowly. "I'm having a nice time. But it sounds like you already have the summer planned. I'm not really looking to lock into any kind of serious relationship."

His heart sank. "Oh. Well, forget I said anything then." He tried to cover it up with a smile. "I say stuff all the time. It doesn't mean anything."

"No, it clearly means something." She spoke slowly and tried to choose her words carefully. "I don't want you to think that this is more serious than it actually is."

Craig's brain shut down and he immediately began to ramble in a futile attempt to save the date. "Hey, I'm as cool as a cucumber. We can move at whatever pace you want. It's not like I'm falling in love with you. Okay, I am really getting strong feelings, but that doesn't mean I'm falling in love. That's way down the line, right? Like, maybe we're aiming for that, but that doesn't mean we're there now."

Amanda retrieved her purse reluctantly. "I really should get going."

"No, no! Don't leave like that. I'm freaking you out. I'm sorry. That's…it's not who I am. Maybe I'm a little nervous. I haven't really felt anything for anyone since my wife passed away, and I feel a really strong connection with you." *Craig, you're making this worse. Stop talking, please. You're losing her.*

She took his hand and held it with both of hers. "You're a wonderful guy, Craig. But I think we're a bad fit. It's bad timing, that's all. I really had a nice time, though."

He sat in stunned silence.

"How much do I owe you for the lunch?" She slid her hand into her purse.

Swallowing hard, he shook his head. "No, don't worry about that. It's taken care of. Really. Thanks for offering."

"Okay." She smiled again and tortured him with the look that had caught his attention in the first place before she turned and left.

Nice work, Craig. You had a wonderful woman right there, ready to date you, and you scared her off. He slumped his shoulders and leaned back against the iron patio chair to rock morosely. When she drove past in her car and waved to him, he straightened quickly, smiled, and waved in response so she wouldn't see him in pain.

Once she was out of sight, he put his elbows on the table and buried his face in his hands. *You have completely forgotten how to date. That's why this went so poorly. It's not because there aren't great women out there or even good fits for you. You simply have no clue what you're doing anymore. You're trying to act like you can replace Carol right off the bat, but you built your relationship with her over years and years of dating and shared experiences. Why do you fall into this trap?*

Fighting the urge to shed any tears in public, Craig cleaned their plates quickly and hurried to the SUV. He closed the door behind him and started the engine before he leaned his head back on the headrest and closed his eyes.

"Craig Watson, still the master at ruining dates. Carol was a godsend, man. No one else will tolerate you."

As he sank into a deep depression, he thrust the car into Drive and headed home, where he could hole up away from public view for a while.

CHAPTER NINETEEN

A feeling of dread accompanied Vickie when she walked through the doors of Al's Seafood. As she slipped her punch card into the machine to time-stamp it, she knew it would be a rough day.

But it wasn't a feeling of pending danger or doom. It was a stack of boxes she saw as she walked around the back of the building.

"Good afternoon." Steve greeted her with a smile. "I have a special job for you today."

Ugh. I hate that smile. I know what it means. He's joking, but still. "Yeah, I saw them already."

He folded his hands in front of his body and bounced on his heels. "You're getting the hang of this place. I love that I don't have to give you so much direction anymore."

She retrieved a navy-blue apron from the row of hooks near the back door and slipped the top loop over her head. "Well, it seems simple enough. All I have to do is remember that I'm in charge of doing all the jobs no one else wants to do."

Steve uttered a belly laugh. "Now, now...there's a hier-archy that everyone follows. The next time we hire some-one, you'll be relieved of those duties. It's simply how things work here."

"But until then..." She caught the loose ends of the apron and tied them around her waist while she rolled her eyes dramatically.

"Until then, you're in charge of it. Yep. Look, everyone who works here has had to go through what you're going through." He looked over his shoulder at the other two women. Patti stood at the front of the store and counted the money in the register, while Crystal removed the plastic wrap that covered the various bowls of deli salads. "I think that's why Crystal is so nice to you. She had to do all that stuff before you were hired."

"Yup!" the woman called from the deli counter. "Thanks for giving me a break, Vickie."

Everyone chuckled, except Vickie, who didn't say another word before she pushed the back door open and walked out to the stack of boxes beside the outdoor freezer. She stood in front of them and sighed.

This was one of the more peculiar jobs at Al's Seafood. Inside those various boxes were different kinds of fish—cod, shrimp, walleye, and anything else on the menu. Some boxes had individually wrapped fish, and others simply had big plastic bags full of fish chunks flash-frozen so they wouldn't stick together.

In the system that Al's Seafood operated under, containers of fish needed to be easily accessible on a moment's notice. When he first explained it to her, Steve was adamant that this was the only way to go.

"I know it seems pointless to unpack the fish from these boxes and put them into other containers, but during a Friday night fish fry, every second you save counts. The last thing you want to do when you're buried eight- or nine-deep in the store is to have to tear boxes open and fiddle with plastic bags. By doing it this way, it's a grab 'n go operation and it's way faster."

The vampire understood the logic to a point, but that didn't make the job any less tedious. She took a pair of gloves off the hook beside the freezer door and slipped them on her hands. Once she'd wiggled her fingers to settle them in place, she took a razor blade from her back pocket and dragged it across the tape of the first box in front of her.

She pulled the flaps open and broke the rest of the tape that secured it. Inside was a large plastic bag with a knot tied in it. Large white chunks of frozen fish greeted her.

"Oh, shoot." She walked back to the store and opened the back door. Without stepping inside, she hauled a stack of big blue plastic bins from the bottom shelf of the unit inside the door.

Back at the freezer, she separated one of the bins from the stack and dropped it onto the pavement. She cut the plastic bag with the razor blade to open a large enough hole that she could pour the fish into the bin.

At least you know what you're doing. Remember when you were caught untying each of the bags? Jason had a field day making fun of you for that for some reason.

The chunks of fish slid into the box like a pile of bricks. Vickie leaned down and spread the contents until the layer was flat in the bin. She had room for one more.

A hasty scan of the stack of boxes located another matching package and she repeated the process to fill the bin until it was almost overflowing. *Only enough room for two more pieces.*

With a sigh, she tugged on the handle to open the walk-in freezer. A blast of frigid air all but knocked her back. She picked up the heavy bin of frozen fish and ducked her head to step through the hanging plastic slats that kept too much cold air from escaping. Quickly, she slid the bin onto a rack on the left side of the freezer and walked out into the sunny, beautiful spring day.

This job is so much easier when I can use my powers. Everything is. If this is what it's like to be a human, I don't know that I want to do it. This sure is annoying.

As always, whenever she fell into a funk like this, she simply reminded herself of the promise she made to Craig —that no matter what, she wouldn't use her powers. She would keep her word.

One by one, she ripped boxes open, tossed their contents into bins, and slid them into the freezer. It was a classic "new guy" job—useful enough to be annoying but worthless enough to make you question its purpose.

Vickie tried to do the best she could with it. She'd try to see how quickly she could fill a bin. But there weren't many ways to dress up such a tedious, menial task.

As she hoisted a bin full of raw jumbo shrimp into the freezer, she paused and her stomach twisted. *Uh oh. What's going on? Who's around? Is something going to happen to me? No, that's not it. Danger is lurking, but I don't know where.*

She tried to shake it off. It didn't matter anyway because she couldn't use her powers. But she wondered if someone was out in the street in front of the store and perhaps in danger of being struck by a car. That was an all too common occurrence, or so the news reports suggested. Of course, it could only seem that way because bad news was in demand, so that was all they ever talked about.

The vampire stepped away from the freezer and peeked through the slats of the fence that separated her from street view. Anyone driving past would not see workers from Al's Seafood unloading boxes.

She squinted through the slats in both directions but saw no one in the street. *That is so weird. Usually, this feeling means the danger is nearby. But what could possibly be close to me?*

What she failed to realize was that the store had opened and someone had walked in brandishing a gun.

It didn't take long for the man to make himself known. He walked up to the register and pointed it at Patti, who caught her breath when she saw it.

"Can… Can I help you?"

The man wore no expression that might indicate his state of mind. Despite holding a gun out in the open, he kept his voice low so he would not draw attention to himself. "Open the register." His voice was measured and almost calm.

Patti's heart raced. A bead of sweat ran down her temple as she pushed the button to open the register drawer. She glanced at her coworkers, who were all frozen in place.

From his position at the back of the store, Steve stared at Patti but he couldn't say a word. *Do what we were all trained to do, Patti. Cooperate with him. No sudden movements.*

Let the cops deal with him. He turned his gaze to the camera over the register area, satisfied that it would obtain a clear image of the criminal.

Outside, Vickie emerged from the freezer and moved forward to fill another bin of cod when she looked across the walkway and into one of the windows of the store. To her shock, she saw the man with the gun.

She, too, froze in place.

If I could tap into my speed, I could take care of that guy without anyone knowing what happened. I could move fast enough that they wouldn't even see me. But I can't use my powers. I run the risk of being caught. Come on, Patti, don't do anything foolish. Cooperate with the guy. Man, I wish I could be in there to stop this.

The vampire watched helplessly as everything unfolded.

Inside, Patti withdrew stacks of bills and placed them on the counter. The robber picked them up with his left hand and tucked them into the inside breast pocket of the jacket he wore.

The woman trembled with fear and did everything she could to not burst into tears. Her hands shook, however, and she dropped a stack of ten-dollar bills onto the floor, where they scattered. Her coworkers held a collective breath.

"Sorry!" She stooped to pick them up.

"No! Leave them." The gunman gritted his teeth. He didn't know if this was a ruse or not and he had no desire to find out. "Leave them down there."

"I can—"

Patti straightened and placed some of the bills on the

counter. Before she could bend again, the man pulled the trigger.

At the sharp report, everyone gasped. Outside, Vickie's eyes widened. *Was Patti actually shot?*

The bullet lodged itself into the woman's left shoulder. She stumbled back and slumped into a seated position on the floor. Frantically, the gunman slid all the bills on the counter together, scooped them up, and ran out the door to a waiting car. The tires squealed as he made his escape.

Vickie sprinted into the store and froze when she saw Patti on the floor in a blood-stained shirt. Crystal and Steve ran to her to make sure she was okay and the woman sobbed loudly in excruciating pain.

"You're okay. You're okay." Crystal knelt beside her and held her hand.

Once Steve was satisfied that she was reasonably safe, he retrieved his cell phone to dial nine-one-one. He marched to the back of the store so he could hear the operator on the other line. When he saw Vickie who had finally managed to take a step forward, he moved the phone away from his ear. "Patti was shot. Go lock the door to make sure no one can get in right now. I'll call the police and an ambulance."

Without questioning it, she jogged through the back of the store, around the deli counter, and to the front door. She flipped the deadbolt and pulled the chain to turn off the *OPEN* sign. She was about to check on Patti when Steve shouted from the back. "Stay at the door. You need to let the police in when they get here in a minute."

A lump formed in her throat while she stood there helplessly and listened to her coworker's pained moans.

She could have done something to help, but without using her powers, she had no opportunity to do so.

I could have stopped this from happening. But I didn't. I was stuck. And now, she's been seriously hurt.

Once the paramedics loaded Patti onto a stretcher—thankfully no longer writhing in pain—the vampire choked tears back while the woman was wheeled out of the store. She caught her hand, her voice small and weak. "I'm so sorry."

Patti had received a shot of morphine so they could transport her. She shook her head quickly. "It wasn't your fault. Don't worry about it."

She covered her mouth with both hands while they loaded the patient into the ambulance and drove away. Steve hastily scribbled a sign indicating that the store was closed for an emergency situation and taped it to the inside of the door. He flipped the deadbolt again.

"I'm closing for the day. If you want to stay and help, that's fine. But I don't mind if you're too shaken up."

Crystal and Vickie opted to stay and help clean up, cover the deli containers, and move the still-boxed fish into the freezer before it was ruined.

He shook his head as he wheeled a mop and bucket to the front of the store. "This lousy neighborhood." His face settled into a scowl as he squeezed the water out of the mop and began to clean the blood.

CHAPTER TWENTY

F rustration mounted for Jim Trembo, who continued his apparently futile prowl through the corridors of Clear Lake High School. He tugged at the lanyard around his neck. *Cheesy little thing. I feel like I'm back in high school myself.* At the end of the lanyard was a laminated card with his photo on it and a barcode on the back.

It was his ID, signifying that he was, at least for the moment, considered a member of the staff of the high school. He sneered at the photo. *My smile looks stupid. It's a good thing I don't really have to show this to anyone.*

The ID was merely a formality. Mr Goede had thought of every way to enable him to assimilate as quickly as possible. And while the principal was in full support of cooperation with the agent, he still watched him from time to time, puzzled at what he actually looked for.

He'd watch Jim pace through one or other of the hallways and glance at the plaques and trophies on display. Or he would slip into the Art Hall to view some of the latest projects completed by students.

While he couldn't necessarily doubt the man's intentions, he certainly wondered about his tactics.

What he didn't know was that Jim was, basically, bored out of his mind. For two full weeks, he'd maintained his daily patrol of Clear Lake High School and accomplished absolutely nothing of any value.

His problem stemmed from one simple fact—he didn't know what or who he was looking for.

This problem was heightened whenever the bell rang and kids poured into the hallways. He'd shuffle to the side so everyone could move freely, but he never saw any evidence of odd or suspicious activity. There was nothing signifying anything even remotely out of the ordinary.

Clearly, his apparently clever plan had a major flaw.

I need to think of a way to weed these kids out and ignore the ones who have nothing to do with this situation.

One day, he had something of a breakthrough. He saw a blonde girl strolling down the hall on the way to her next class and she wore a pink cross country sweatshirt—the same type that was seen in the video.

Jim's heart surged and he immediately bolted toward the girl. He tapped her on the shoulder and she turned to him with wide eyes. "Yes?"

"Can you please step aside and speak to me?"

"Oh…kay…" She stepped cautiously to one side of the hallway and stared at this brute of a man with obvious nervousness. "Am I in trouble?"

He smiled at her. "No, you're not. But I think you can help me. Are you a member of the cross country team?"

The girl looked at the shirt. "Oh. No, I'm not. I borrowed this from my friend Natalie."

"How many of these shirts are there?"

"I don't know." She shrugged vaguely. "One for every member of the cross country team, I guess?"

She's a blonde, so she's not from the video. And she's borrowed the shirt, so she probably doesn't know that much about the cross country team, either. "Okay, you can head off to class. Thank you."

Quickly, she scurried off to get as far away from him as possible.

The bell rang and the halls emptied once again. His mind began to race. *If I can only see these girls running—see them in action—maybe I could pick out the suspicious ones.*

Jim made a beeline for Mr Goede's office, knocked on the door, and immediately let himself in.

Inside, the principal huddled over the phone in conversation with one of the parents. He gave the intruder an annoyed look and raised his finger to let him know he had to wait a while.

He nodded and took a seat in one of the chairs. After a quick exchange, the man hung up the phone and turned to face him.

"Mr Trembo, before you say anything, I want to know what your plan is."

"My plan?"

"Yes. I've begun to feel as though you are not operating with any kind of game plan. I'm happy to give you access to the school, but we need to organize this effort a little better. Otherwise, you're merely a strange man wandering the halls of my school, and that doesn't sit well with me."

"I totally understand what you are saying, sir. I actually

have some ideas about that. I spoke to a young girl today—"

"Without my involvement? Jim, that wasn't a part of the deal. You aren't supposed to interact with the kids on your own."

"Relax. It was out in the open, surrounded by other kids, and it lasted all of fifteen seconds."

Skeptical, Mr Goede looked down his nose at him. "And?"

"She says these pink cross country sweatshirts are given to everyone in the cross country team. Is that correct?"

"Um, I assume so. I don't keep track of that particular one. But there are many of those around. Why?"

Jim leaned forward. "That sweatshirt is what I'm looking for. Do you have a yearbook I can use?"

The principal shook his head apologetically. "We don't have this year's one ready. You could look at last year's, but I don't know how that would help you. What do you need a yearbook for?"

"I want to know who the cross country athletes are. I have a strong suspicion about that, so I want to observe a practice or a race or something that will let me see if they display signs of any unfair advantages."

He had adopted that term to explain what he was looking for without stating his longing to discover supernatural activity.

"The cross country season is over, Jim. That's in the fall."

"Okay, so what other way can I use to see those on the cross country team this year in action?" He folded his arms.

"I suppose you could talk to Coach Lueck. He would

have a roster of some kind, I'm sure. But you still wouldn't see them in action. Do they need to run for you?"

"What do you mean?"

"We have other sports, and most of the cross country runners are still involved in something. Soccer, softball, track, that kind of thing."

"That's better than nothing. Sure. You have a schedule for that, I assume?"

"Of course. I can send that to you." He tapped his keyboard. "That's odd."

"What?" Jim prepared himself for the possibility that something was wrong on the computer and he wouldn't get any answers that day.

"Oh, nothing. I merely find it funny that you're looking for performance-enhancing drugs in the most strait-laced sports team we have here at Clear Lake."

"Hormone treatments and other drugs can aid runners in accomplishing great feats, sir. It's not out of the realm of possibility."

The principal scooted his chair to the printer and retrieved a schedule for the rest of the month. "Here are the games scheduled from now until the end of the year."

"Is there one team that is more likely to have former cross country runners on it? Would there be a good place for me to focus my efforts?"

"I can't say. There are many runners on the track team, but as many on softball. Since I don't know what you're looking for, that's the best help I can give you. If your intention is to analyze their play, you'll probably have to go to all these events. If you only select one or two, you might pick the wrong one and waste your time."

Jim nodded briskly and took the sheet of paper with the schedule off the desk. He told himself he would get to work and attend some of the games and meets, hoping that would bring him closer to the supernatural being.

Before he made it out the door, Mr Goede stopped him. "Hey, Jim?"

"Yeah?"

"Who did you talk to today? Who told you about the cross country team and everything?"

He released the doorknob. "Well, first of all, I don't know who. I never asked her name. Second, I want there to be some distance between you and the student in question. I'm trying to limit the variables in this entire investigation."

The principal remained at his desk and fumed. *This guy wants access to everything—including girls' sports—and won't include me in the monitoring of his own activity. It really rubs me the wrong way.*

With the schedule tucked away in his pocket, Jim Trembo resumed his pretend duties with new confidence. When classes finished, the hallways overflowed with students once again. To add realism to his status, he paid attention to another hall monitor who worked very hard to keep the kids intimidated by her.

A thin black woman—he believed he'd heard she was a former police officer—stood motionless on one side of the lobby. She folded her arms across her chest and adopted an expression that sent shivers up the spines of the students. With her eyes half-open, she stared at them, her jaw clenched as she looked down her nose at everyone.

Jim didn't want to completely rip her off, but it would make sense that the other hall monitor would act in a similar way. He didn't adopt the strong, angry face, but he did stand tall and confidently, knowing that he had the power to break fights up and send kids to detention should they break the rules.

Of course, he had no interest in any of those things. All he wanted to do was find the supernatural being masquerading as a high school student. He would leave the rest up to the real hall monitor to take care of.

Now, he simply needed to wait out the rest of the day, after which he would plan to attend a few sporting events over the weekend.

As he stood there, he thought about the anxious tone in Mr Goede's voice. He knew the man's patience was wearing thin. His only hope was to find this girl as quickly as possible so he could take custody of the being before the school administration tried to get in his way.

CHAPTER TWENTY-ONE

The meager crowd cheered and clapped while the young woman who hit the ball rounded first base and paused to see where the ball had ended up before running to second. She decided to stay at first, and the crowd continued to cheer their approval for a solid base hit to kick off the game.

It was a beautiful afternoon, but earlier girls' softball games tended to be not as well-attended as later ones. Still, for Vickie, Eric, Alexis, and Charlie, it was the perfect low-pressure double date for the four of them to enjoy a little time together.

The date was new territory for everyone. For Alexis, this was the chance to date a guy who didn't want to kill her by draining the blood from her neck. And from a social standpoint, he was a friendly, outgoing, popular boy instead of a quiet, boring, brooding one.

For Vickie and Eric, it was an opportunity to spend time together without the pressure of their previous conversation. He still didn't buy that everything was on the up and up and believed that she was still hiding something about that video. She felt the pressure of lying to her boyfriend, and that affected her behavior around him.

The only person involved in the date who didn't feel awkward was Charlie. He was happy to be there and as he had told his date many times in the past, he didn't do awkward.

Still, everything started out pleasantly enough, and the game kicked off with a good burst of action. The Clear Lake girls scored a run in the first inning off a series of hits, which allowed everyone to get a little more comfortable before they really felt like they were on a date.

Charlie kept up most of the conversation at the beginning and commented on a few of the girls on the team and funny things they had done in class.

"Oh, man, Tina's up to bat. She's cool. I remember she did a presentation in our history class and I don't even remember what it was for. But as her visual aid, she took a baseball bat and smashed a mirror. It was awesome, but I don't think Mr Tatge knew she would do that. Glass went everywhere. There were supposed to be two other presentations that day, but she had to spend the rest of the time cleaning glass up that scattered all over the classroom. It was crazy."

Thank goodness for Charlie right now. He's keeping this date going. Eric continued to be distracted by the prospect of Vickie being in that video. He merely didn't know how else to approach her. *She told me she wasn't and I have to believe her. But come on, that rip in her sweatshirt? That's a dead giveaway. She has to be involved in this. But she wouldn't lie to me. Would she?*

Charlie patted him on the shoulder and stood on the bleachers. "Ladies, do you want something to drink? Eric and I are buying." He winked at the other boy who smiled in response and nodded. After getting an order for a round of Pepsis, the two boys descended and walked to the concession stand.

"I can buy if you weren't prepared to pay. I didn't mean to put you on the spot."

"No, no, it's fine. I have money." Eric shrugged.

"Cool. So what's your story, man? We don't really know each other. How long have you and Vickie been going out?"

He turned and looked at the girls, who were huddled close and talked to each other. "I don't know. Seven or eight months?"

"Nice. Things are going well, then."

"Yeah. I guess. It's…um, yeah. I guess."

"Okay." *Maybe he's a little shy.* The boys ordered their drinks when they reached the front of the line and waited. "What do you like to do for fun? I know you're on the cross country team, right?"

"Yep. I run cross country in the fall. Um, I don't do all that much for fun. I hang out with my family or watch YouTube."

"Cool. What kinds of stuff? I think those *Dude Perfect* guys are hilarious."

Eric shook his head. "I don't think I've ever watched them."

Charlie laughed. "They're simply a group of idiots who do stunts and trick shots and stuff. It sounds lame unless you actually watch it. Look them up sometime. What do you watch, then?"

They took their sodas and turned to head back. "I watch old commercials."

"Commercials?"

"Yeah. From, like, the eighties and nineties."

"Why?"

"I like them. They're fun. Different. Kinda like a snapshot of a simpler time."

"Okay, okay. That's cool." *Kinda weird, but hey, we are all a little weird.*

Back at the bleachers, the girls were waiting—and Vickie felt awful.

"Are you all right?" Alexis asked her. "You look like you're ready to puke."

"No. I won't puke, but I'm not okay." She tried to clutch her stomach subtly. "Something's off. I can't seem to really figure out what's bothering me. Remember when I told you and your dad that something worse was coming?"

Her sister nodded. "Worse than the Circle. Yeah, I remember."

"It's still coming. I don't know what it is but it's still coming, and it's getting closer. It scares the living daylights out of me, and I don't know what to do about it."

"Can you...I don't know..." Her voice trailed off. "Is there a place you can go? Or explore?"

The vampire gave her an exasperated look. "I don't know. I would go out into the field because I know there's something out there. But it's a public space and I can't use my powers in public anymore. It keeps me from being able to do anything because I'm worried I'll be stuck in a bad situation that I can't get myself out of."

Alexis took a deep breath. "Have you talked to my dad about it?"

"What's there to talk about? He's right. I can't use my powers anywhere. It'll only get me in trouble."

"So your plan is to ignore your crippling anxiety for the rest of your life?" The girl smirked at her. "That ain't gonna work."

"I know it won't. But I also don't know what else to do." She ran her fingers through her hair. "What's worse is that the feeling is getting stronger at school."

Before Alexis could respond, the boys returned with their sodas. The girls thanked them, and the four of them resumed watching the game.

Vickie hoped the soda would somehow settle her stomach, but her instincts were too strong. They had pushed through even stronger now, to the point that she wore a pained look on her face.

Eric glanced over and noticed it. "Hey, are you okay?"

She forced a smile. "I'm fine. Girl stuff." *That one always works.*

Sure enough, he nodded and refused to bring it up again. Girl stuff was something he never wanted to hear anything about.

Charlie nodded toward another set of bleachers, where a tall man in a shirt and tie sat on the top bench. "Hey, isn't that the new hall monitor?"

The group looked over. Sure enough, Jim Trembo sat with a notebook and pen and followed the girls' softball game closely.

JUDITH BERENS

"That dude is weird." Charlie shook his head. "I don't know if he's simply giving a vibe off or what, but he is not normal."

"Forget about normal," Alexis chimed in, "why is he even here? What school adds a second hall monitor a month before the end of the school year? Seriously, what's his purpose?"

"I heard there was some kind of violent incident between two students that the school has kept under wraps," Eric told them. "They apparently hired this guy to keep the peace for the rest of the year. He's a former Navy SEAL. I know these are all rumors, but it would make sense."

"Dang." Charlie turned to him. "But if that were true, I feel like we'd all know about whoever was stabbed or whatever. If there was a violent incident at school, word would spread. It's kinda like that time that one kid peed his pants in Spanish class. That made the rounds by the end of the day. If a dude was stabbed? I bet we'd all know about it."

Everyone nodded and returned their attention to the game. Vickie, however, still stared at Trembo and wondered why she had such a bad feeling from him.

Alexis leaned over and whispered in her ear. "Hey. You're on a date. Do you want to act like it?"

"I will." She took a deep breath and tried to focus her attention on the date and the game.

Still, she couldn't shake her feeling of dread. The new hall monitor guy distracted her simply by being there. *Is he why I've felt so lousy lately? If so, what's his deal? Why is he here scribbling notes at a girls' softball game?*

Trembo hunched over his pocket notebook, listened to the announcements over the PA system, and noted each batter and their performance. He looked frustrated and disappointed as though things hadn't gone the way he wanted them to.

Eric tapped her on the shoulder. "Do you wanna go for a walk?" He leaned over to Alexis and Charlie. "We'll be right back."

"Stay where we can see you," Charlie joked and chuckled.

The couple walked to a nearby playground. Normally, kids would swarm the playset while their older sisters would be on the field playing softball. But that afternoon, no one was there.

They sat on the swings and swayed lazily back and forth.

"Something's wrong with you." He broke the silence after a while and she didn't argue. "Are you okay? What is weighing on you this much?"

"It's nothing. I can't really talk about it."

"Is it school? Is it home? Does it have to do with the conversation we had?"

"No. It's none of that, really. I'm simply preoccupied with a few things right now. I'm fine." She took his hand gently. "We're good. You and me, we're totally one hundred percent good. I'm not worried about the conversation we had. It's simply the end of the year thing, I guess. Summer's coming up and I have so much on my plate."

He nodded. It was a good enough excuse that he didn't need to dig any further. While he held her hand, though, his brain begged him to ask her about the rip in her sweatshirt. *If you ask her about that, you might corner her into admitting that it's her in the video. But she also could totally break up with you if you push it. That would show that you don't trust her word. So keep your mouth shut, man. Let it be whatever it is. You have a good thing going. Don't screw it up.*

After a few more seconds of awkward pauses, they agreed to go back to the bleachers and resume watching the game. They tried to have a good time, but her gaze strayed constantly to the new hall monitor. Whatever he was doing there really bothered her. Worse, she was afraid to find out what it all meant.

CHAPTER TWENTY-TWO

The girls returned home that evening after the game a little after dinnertime. When they walked in the door, Alexis was in a bouncing good mood. She was getting along great with Charlie, and it was still a little hard for her to believe that she was dating such a popular guy.

"It's not only that he's popular, it's that he's a total sweetheart," she explained as they walked in the side door of the house. "Maybe I'm biased because the last guy I dated tried to kill me. Anyway, it's a good thing they had hot dogs at the game because this would be way too late for dinner."

"Yeah." Vickie was a little on the morose side but tried not to take her bad mood out on the other girl. *She's simply in a happy place. It's not her fault you're dealing with all this. Let her be happy.* "Hot dogs don't usually fill me up but tonight, they were perfect. I'll head off to bed."

"Already?" Alexis looked at the clock on the wall in the kitchen. "It's only seven o'clock."

"I'm tired. I think I need to unwind and relax—as much as I can, anyway."

"How are you feeling?" She put her hand on her sister's shoulder. "Do you feel bad right now?"

The vampire inhaled deeply and walked over to the patio door to stare out into the field. "I feel a sense of dread, but I'm not in pain. It's…fine. This is about as relaxed as I get nowadays. I'm merely drained, I guess."

"Okay. Well, get some rest. I'll see you in the morning."

"G'night." She disappeared into the dark house and wandered down the hallway to her room.

"Dad, are you around?" Alexis called into the darkness. She flipped the light switch next to the sink and filled a glass with water, drank it quickly, and put it on the countertop. *His SUV is in the driveway and the door was unlocked, so I know he's home. It sure is quiet around here, though.*

She walked into the living room, turned the lamp on, and jumped when she saw her father seated in his recliner, alone in the quiet darkness. "Jeez, Dad! What are you doing sitting around by yourself like this? You scared the crap out of me."

"Sorry, baby." His eyes were bloodshot, and his face was sullen. "How was the game?"

"It was fine. What is wrong with you?"

"Nothing, sweetheart." He pushed himself up so he sat straight and tried to ease the grief from his face. After blinking a few times, he looked at her with a weak smile. "I was thinking. So you had fun, huh? Did we win?"

"Yeah."

"Good. How is the new boy?"

"He's good." Alexis looked at the glass in his hand. "Dad, are you drinking?"

He sniffed and looked at the ice cube that swirled in his almost-empty glass. "Only one. I had a long day. Don't worry about it. I've had scotch plenty of times."

Warily, she walked over to the other recliner and sat. "Yeah, but you don't drink by yourself in the dark."

He snickered. "You're making it sound like I'm an alcoholic."

"Maybe I should show you a mirror. You look like an alcoholic. But I know you're not. What's wrong?"

He shook his head and said nothing. *The last thing you want to do is burden your child with your own sob stories. That's not her place. Man up and keep it to yourself.*

"Dad, seriously. Talk to me."

"You're my daughter. This isn't something you need to concern yourself with."

She crossed her legs and extended her arms to gesture to the rest of the living room. "Hey, Dad, look around you for a second. Do you see Mom around?"

Confused, he looked around and then at her again. "No, Mom isn't here, honey."

Alexis dropped her hands into her lap. "Exactly. Everyone needs to talk to someone sometime. You haven't worked outside the house in forever. You aren't going out with any buddies. And you don't have a wife to confide in anymore. If you keep everything inside, it'll kill you. You need someone to talk to. And since I'm the only one here, I guess you're stuck with talking to me until you can find a replacement."

He looked into her eyes and she didn't back down.

Instead, she stared at him with as much determination as ever. *She has that same spunk Carol did. Doggone it.*

Craig laughed at his daughter. "You don't take no for an answer, do you?"

She smiled. "Did Mom?"

"No. No, she didn't." He sighed. "How's Vickie doing?"

"You're changing the subject."

"We'll come back to me. How is she? She's had a rough few weeks."

Alexis tilted her head. "Yeah, something is definitely up with her. I know she's bothered by not being able to use her powers. That incident at the grocery store shook her a little, but I know that the robbery at work really set her off. I think she's carrying too many burdens on her shoulders. And on top of that, she says something bad is going to happen but she can't pinpoint what that is."

"The poor girl." He took a sip of his scotch. "You know, everyone dreams about having super-powers, but here's someone who has been blessed with some really powerful abilities, and they've become something that causes more complications than anything else."

"Exactly." She nodded. "I think because she's the only one who has these powers, she feels like she has the responsibility to make sure bad things don't happen to anyone ever. And now that she isn't allowed to use them, she feels handcuffed."

"Well, she'll be handcuffed for real if she's caught using them."

She clapped her hands. "Okay, now let's get back to you."

"Honey, it's only a dating thing. You wouldn't understand."

"I wouldn't understand?" She put her hand on her chest, almost offended.

"Sorry, I don't want to be rude. You've started dating a good guy. It's not like you're a well-versed expert in the field of romance."

"Okay, maybe I don't know everything there is to know about relationships, but I know girls."

"Girls. I'm talking about women here."

His daughter laughed in disbelief. "Give me a break, Dad. It's not nearly as different as you think. Besides, I'm not saying I can sit here and fix everything for you. But I can give you a perspective that you probably need. And if nothing else, you can get some of this off your chest. Otherwise, you'll simply try to drink it away, and that definitely won't work."

Craig cleared his throat. *She sure knows how to debate these things.* "Fine. I botched my date with Amanda today, okay?"

"What did you do?"

"I don't know. One minute, we're joking around and talking about future dates, the next minute, she's telling me it won't work out and ditches me in the middle of our lunch."

"Hmm." Alexis frowned thoughtfully. "Did you both talk about future dates or only you?"

He thought back to the date itself. "I guess it was only me."

"You probably put too much pressure on her." She took

pity on her dad. "Pop, you can't do that so quickly. You'd only been on one date with her. You have to chill out."

"But that date went so well."

"Right. But if a date goes well, it can always be a fluke. Women know that good guys are hard to find."

"Aren't I a good guy?"

"Dad, you're the best guy. But that's not the point. Anyone can seem like a good guy on one date. She was still feeling you out to make sure you would be a good fit for her. If you came on too strongly, that probably scared her off."

Craig groaned. "It's hard to play it cool."

"Of course it is because you haven't had to for a long time. You and Mom were always so affectionate towards each other."

He smiled wistfully. "I miss that. We could hold hands, kiss whenever we wanted to, and pat each other on the butt. Anytime I needed a little physical contact, I could simply wrap my arms around your mom."

"I know. It was gross." She smiled and laughed. "But you built your way up to that. You're not at that stage with anyone now. You're starting over from scratch."

"I don't want to start over. I want to move at the pace I want."

"Yeah, well, that's not an option. And you'll have to get over that very quickly. Women at your age are probably starting over, too. Was Amanda coming away from a serious relationship?"

Craig nodded. "A marriage. They had a kid and he left her."

"Okay, huge. She's going through the same things you

are. But instead of being desperate for affection, she has her guard up. She's worried that she'll choose the wrong person and she doesn't want to be hurt again. Her stakes are different than your stakes. And if you want to keep a relationship going, you'll have to work with her stakes."

"So I have to take it slow?" He almost looked aggrieved.

"Well, yeah. You have to take it slow so you can get a feel for where that person's head is at. It sounds like the ship with Amanda has sailed. But the next relationship you come across, start with her in mind. Don't worry about what you want out of it. You'll get there. Start with her."

"I wish I hadn't screwed it up with her. She was perfect." He hung his head.

"No, she wasn't, Dad. You know how I know?"

"How?"

"Because she's not here. She got up and left. That's how I know she wasn't perfect for you. If she was perfect, you two would be together right now. It's okay. It's her loss."

He polished off the rest of his scotch and placed the glass on the coaster next to him. "How do you find the perfect woman?"

"You do the same thing that you told me—you don't look for her. Simply make yourself available. You ran into this girl at the auto shop. There are plenty of other fish in the sea who you'll run into. Don't sweat it so much. You're a good guy. The right woman is out there, waiting for you to sweep her off her feet. And if you take your time with her, she'll turn into the affectionate woman you're looking for. I promise."

Craig choked down the lump in his throat and looked at his daughter with tears in his eyes. "You're a smart girl."

"I know." She laughed.

"Thanks, sweetheart."

She stood from her chair, patted him on the knee, and took the glass. "You can watch TV if you want. Get your mind off this and relax a little. But you're done drinking tonight."

"Yes, ma'am." He picked the remote up and turned the TV on, amused at his daughter's forcefulness. *When she knows the right thing to do, she doesn't let up. She'll be okay.*

CHAPTER TWENTY-THREE

At the concession stand, Alexis was tempted to start acting like she used to. "Don't make me turn into an eight-year-old again, Dad."

Craig laughed at his daughter as he retrieved his wallet. "Don't you have a job now? Buy your own candy bars."

"I didn't bring any cash. Come on, I'll pay you back. And I don't want a candy bar, I want a bag of Skittles."

He shook his head with amusement. "You and your Skittles. Fine, throw 'em on."

"Yes!" She pumped her fist and grabbed a king-sized bag of the sugary treats.

While they paid, Pete Stabone stood behind them and smirked at the father-daughter interaction. It made him miss his family, who waited patiently for him to finish this investigation and return to them in Virginia. Watching another father and daughter was the closest thing he had to that, for now at least.

They remind me of me and Wendy. That girl can get me to

buy anything. He folded his arms and waited patiently for his turn.

After they paid, Craig turned and rolled his eyes at Pete. "Sorry to hold the line up. My daughter has a way."

He laughed. "I understand completely. I was thinking how much she reminds me of my daughter. You held on far longer than I ever could."

They shared a laugh and father and daughter headed to the bleachers. Pete bought himself a bag of popcorn and a soda and climbed to the top of the bleachers where Jim sat with a notebook on his knee.

But while the softball game had kept him somewhat entertained, that evening bored him. "Track meets are dull. I never realized it."

His colleague sat next to him. "They can be. There's merely a lot of bouncing around to different groups. If you don't know enough kids, most of the stuff won't interest you."

"And if you don't know any of the kids, it makes you want to jump off the bleachers head-first so you have something to do."

Pete laughed at the remark and popped a few popcorn kernels into his mouth. "Track is boring, man. Even the races that are fairly exciting are merely people running around a circle."

They watched a freshman boy sprint down the line with a pole in his arms, pierce it into the ground, and use the momentum to hoist himself up and over the bar. He thumped onto the cushion safely while a few people in the crowd cheered.

"See, look at this—pole vaulting." Jim pointed with the

pen in his hand. "When I was younger, this was probably the most exciting thing at a track meet. Now? I am utterly and completely bored."

"Do you want to keep your voice down?" His friend looked around nervously. "That kid's family is probably sitting here somewhere. Don't be rude."

He nodded. *Pete's right. Don't complain too loudly. You're not here to draw attention to yourself. The more you can blend into the background, the better.*

On the other side of the track, four Clear Lake girls, including Krista and Vickie, stretched their legs in preparation for the four-by-four-hundred relay race. Jim Trembo did not blend into the background when it came to the vampire, who stared into the stands at him.

"Is something up?" Krista stepped over to her. "What are you looking at?"

"That hall monitor guy." She nodded in the direction of the bleachers. "What's he doing here?"

"Who knows?" The girl bent forward to touch her toes and stretch her legs. "He's working for the school. Maybe he's here to show a little school spirit. He wants to know more about the place he's working at."

"I guess." *It still bothers me that he takes notes. And I can sense something about him that is throwing me off.*

"Okay, girls!" Coach Lueck clapped briskly as he jogged over to them. "Race time is coming up next. Vickie, I want you to run the last leg. You have good burst, and I want to use that in the home stretch over here. When you round that last turn, I want you to fire up the jets as quickly as you can."

"Yes, sir!" She bounced up and down on her feet as part of her pretense to warm up.

The girls lined up a few minutes later and once the starting gun fired, the race began. The crowd cheered them on as each girl ran her leg of the race and passed the baton to the next one.

As the vampire lined up for her turn, Krista raced towards her. But then Vickie looked over her shoulder at Trembo, who dutifully made notes as he watched the race. *What is he doing? Why is he writing anything down right now? Why does this bother me so much?*

"Vickie! Go, go, go!"

She snapped back to reality to see Krista practically in front of her. She had forgotten to start moving and now, the girl had to slow down to pass the baton. Flustered, she dropped the handoff. From the middle of the field, Coach Lueck uttered an audible groan.

Conscious of how badly she'd messed up, Vickie began to run as quickly as she could without breaking realism. After two hundred meters, she had brought herself to the middle of the pack. At three meters, she fought for the lead.

But as she rounded the last turn, she looked up at the stands, where the mysterious man still scratched his notes, looked at her, and focused on his notebook again. *Is he writing about me? What is he writing? Does he know something? I'd better be careful to not out myself here.*

"Vickie! The jets!" Coach Lueck screamed desperately.

She realized she was at a leisurely jogging pace by now and runners passed her easily. She shook her head and broke into a sprint, managing to finish in third place by the end.

Her teammates were livid and flabbergasted by what had taken place. Krista held them off, then pulled Vickie aside. "What was that?"

"Sorry, I was distracted."

Coach Lueck approached her. "We are lucky that we even came in third place. What happened out there? Do I have to put you in blinders? What were you looking at?"

While she dealt with the fallout of a poor race, Alexis and her dad sat in the bleachers and tried to process what they had seen.

"Surely it can't be because she can't use her powers," he muttered under his breath. "Come on, she has to run faster and be more focused."

"That's what I talked about last night, though. There's something up with her and it's pulling her away from everything." She popped a few Skittles in her mouth and chewed thoughtfully. "I can't put my finger on it. But she was definitely distracted there."

After a few infield events, it was time for the three thousand two hundred meter race.

"All right, this is one we want to watch." Jim scribbled a few notes in his notebook.

"Forgive my ignorance, but why? What's so special about this?" Pete inquired.

"It's a two-mile race. It's only for distance runners. If anyone is on the track team who might also have been on the cross country team, I would bet it's these runners."

He watched eagerly to hear the announcements of the participants in the race. To his surprise, only one runner from Clear Lake was announced. "That's weird."

"What is?" The other man bit into a licorice whip.

"I expected more runners. It sounded like the cross country team and the long-distance runners in track had more overlap but there's only one runner here, though."

He jotted the girl's name down—Tracy Miller. She was a star athlete and she did very well in this particular race. And to his delight, she had a similar build and height to the girl in the viral video.

"I have a good feeling about this one, Pete."

"Are you sure?"

"Trust me. I think that's the girl in the video."

The race started and Tracy ran hard to extend a commanding lead in the very early stages.

But during the sixth lap of the eight required to complete the race, she was tripped by one of her competitors and she fell and landed hard. She managed a partial roll, but she still skidded and sprawled on the track.

At first, the crowd was silent out of concern for the poor girl. But Tracy willed herself to her feet, and she made her way slowly across the finish line.

The crowd cheered for her being able to even finish the race after taking a nasty spill like that.

Even Pete clapped. "She showed a lot of heart out there. Good for her."

Jim shook his head. "She showed more than that, Pete."

"What did she show?"

He pointed at Tracy. "Look at her. We all saw that fall. She skidded along the track. At least some of her skin would have been scraped away. But there's not a scratch on her. She still looks perfect."

"Maybe she simply fell the right way."

He lowered his voice to a whisper. "Maybe. But also, maybe she has the ability to resist that kind of damage."

The other man looked at his colleague, then back at Tracy. "I suppose you're right. Maybe there is more to Tracy Miller than meets the eye."

He scribbled a few more notes, closed his notebook, and slipped it into his pocket. "I think I know who I have to meet next week."

CHAPTER TWENTY-FOUR

Vickie got out of the car and stood in front of the movie theater. It was a beautiful night, but she still felt utterly dejected.

It wasn't that long ago that I was anxious for a date with Eric. It was all I looked forward to. Now, I'm dreading it. I hate lying to him. I hate feeling this way. It's ruining everything.

"Have a good time!" Craig yelled out the window. She waved to him and he drove off.

For a moment, she stayed on the curb in front of the theater. *I can't believe I don't even want to go in. At least it's a movie so we can sit quietly for most of the time. This is so stupid. I love talking to him and laughing with him. That was half the fun of dating. Now, I'm killing time outside instead of running in there to be with him.*

She slapped her thigh and tried to hype herself up before she turned and walked into the theater. Eric waited near the ticket counter with two tickets in his hand and a smile on his face. "Hey! Are you ready to go in?"

"Yep! Let's do it!" She tried to put on a brave face.

After the attendant ripped their tickets, they walked over to the concession stand. "We have a few minutes so we can get popcorn and stuff before heading to Theater Four. What can I get you?"

"Oh, let's see." She stared at the menu. "Yeah, actually, popcorn and a soda would be great."

He gave her a thumbs-up and they stepped into the line to wait their turn. "I'm kinda excited about this movie. When they first announced it, I was like, 'Oh great, another origin story about the Joker.' They've overdone that character so many times."

Eric was a big-time fan of Batman. While he didn't own much Batman-related merchandise and didn't collect toys at his age, he had an appreciation for the character and its world.

"To me, *The Dark Knight* and the whole Nolan trilogy was one of the best things to ever happen to Batman. Like that was the perfect Batman story and nothing will ever top it. And I feel the same about the Joker. Heath Ledger crushed it. Why would anyone try to make that any differently?"

Vickie barely paid attention but nodded here and there to at least seem like she participated in the conversation.

She wasn't entirely successful. He could tell that she wasn't listening but he continued to talk to avoid any awkward pauses. "But when I first saw the trailer for this, I got really mad at myself. Like, 'Shoot, they've gone and done it again. They made one that I'm totally interested in.' I don't think it'll be better than Heath Ledger, but I bet this will be good anyway."

Her expression didn't change at all and disappointed, he

stepped to the front of the line to order their treats.

Once they were armed with a bucket and two sodas, they proceeded to Theater Four.

He continued to avoid the awkward pauses. "The media has been all over this movie, arguing about how bad an influence it'll be on everyone. It's like no one's seen a movie in the last fifty years. Everything is a bad influence. It's fiction."

"Yeah, I know." Tears welled in Vickie's eyes, although she tried to avoid eye contact.

Eric noticed and did his best to ignore it. Mercifully, they reached the theater. They walked in and sat in two reclining seats. Once they were situated, he reached over to lift the armrest between them so they could sit a little closer, but he hesitated when she kept her arm on it and didn't even notice what he tried to do. His stomach sank and he simply faced forward and watched the movie trivia snippets on the big screen.

For several minutes, the two of them stared ahead and did whatever they could to distract themselves from the fact that something was wrong. She worried that things wouldn't work out for them. He wasn't concerned about their relationship and felt it was rock solid. But he also worried that something was wrong and that they wouldn't enjoy the movie with things the way they were.

The previews rolled on and displayed the latest clips from upcoming superhero movies and horror flicks. Neither of them could remember what they were about after they played, as they were both so distracted, they couldn't pay any attention.

The lights finally dimmed and the movie began. The

vampire thought she was disguised by the darkness, and her face twisted into grief and sadness. Her lip quivered, and a few tears rolled down her cheeks. Eric glanced over and saw her crying out of the corner of his eye but didn't know what to do.

He leaned over and whispered in her ear. "Are you okay?"

She looked down. "We need to go talk."

Solemnly, he nodded. They left the popcorn and the sodas at their seats to reserve them for when they returned.

If they returned.

Vickie took him by the hand and led him out of the theater and to the bar set up in the main lobby. They didn't order anything and simply sat at a corner table, as far away from people as possible. She wanted as much privacy as they could get while still staying indoors.

"What is wrong?" He sounded exasperated. "It must be something bad because those tickets cost twelve dollars apiece and we're not in there watching the movie. Are you hurt? Did I do something? Did I say something? What?"

She composed herself, took a few breaths to calm herself, and wiped the tears from her eyes before she spoke in a soft, measured tone. "Do you remember when you asked me about that video you saw online?"

Oh, man. Here it comes. This is it. "Yeah?" *You offended her. She's breaking up with you. It's all over.*

"I need to confess something. That is me in the video."

"Okay. Was this some kind of project you did for school? Or were you simply playing around with video editing software?"

She couldn't help but smile at his feeble attempts to explain the footage away. "No, that's not it. The video is real."

Eric shook his head. "I don't get it. What happened in that video, then?"

This is confession time, Vickie. She took another deep, cleansing breath. *Come clean and hope that he doesn't report you to the government or something crazy like that.* "I need to know that I can trust you. I'm about to tell you something you probably won't believe. It might scare you, and I don't want you to be scared."

"Okay."

"I rescued a dog that would have been hit by a car. I rushed in after the puppy and ran into the car."

"But the vehicle was trashed when it hit you." He frowned in confusion. "How did that happen? What was wrong with that car?"

"There was nothing wrong with it." She stared at the table. "I am able to withstand considerable punishment. I have the ability to run very fast, and my strength can be very...um, strong."

Eric scratched the back of his head. "So...I mean...are you telling me you're some kind of superhero?"

"Not exactly. I'm a vampire."

He released her hand and leaned back in his chair to stare at her, utterly confounded. She studied his face for his reaction and saw one of shock and a trace of fear. "A vampire?"

"Yeah. I'm not a member of Alexis's family. They found me when they were on vacation in Austria. I had been asleep for four hundred years or so. They taught me how to be American and brought me over because my whole family had been killed centuries ago."

Eric looked at the ceiling. "I'm on camera, right? Someone is filming this to get my reaction?"

"No. It's true. I promise you, it's all true."

They were both silent for a moment while the news sank deeper into his brain. "As a vampire, you have super-human abilities, then?"

"I told you about strength and speed. I am also able to absorb information very quickly, and I can sense danger. That's how I knew that dog was about to be run over."

"But...you're a vampire. Are you going to suck my blood?"

The tears had subsided by this point and Vickie could speak more clearly. "No. There were two races of beings in my time—the Sanguinarians and the vampires. Vampires did not suck blood. Sangs did. It was only in pop culture that vampires gained the reputation for drinking blood."

"I only... I... I don't think I really believe this."

"I understand." She smiled and took his hand again. "It's a heavy truth to process. But you can take all the time you need, okay? This doesn't change anything."

He looked at her with disbelief. "This doesn't change anything? You can't be serious. This changes everything."

"And this is why I didn't want to tell you. I don't want you to treat me any differently because I'm a vampire. I am safe to be around. I merely have certain abilities you don't have."

After a moment, he shook his head forcefully. "I don't believe you. This is some kind of prank, and I don't think it's very funny. If that's you in the video, fine. But if you don't want to tell me what really happened, we might as well go back to the movie."

"I am telling you what really happened. Everything you saw was real. All of it."

"Fine." He folded his arms. "Prove it right now. Run around the theater or something. Pick up something over your head. I want to see for myself."

"I can't. I promised Alexis's dad that I wouldn't use my powers anymore. I have healing powers that I've been able to use, but only discreetly. The last time I used my powers, a video of it was plastered all over the news and the Internet. I have stopped using my powers out of necessity because I have to be a normal girl."

Eric stood from his chair. "We need to get back to the movie."

"Are you mad? Are you going to leave me?"

"No. I'm not going to leave you. I think it's a lousy joke but I'm not mad. Besides, like I said, I paid good money for these movie tickets and I'd like to use them, so let's get back in there before we miss too much of the plot."

Vickie obliged and followed him to Theater Four. *Try to understand where he's coming from. You dropped a complete bomb on him. Give him time to process it. Let him know that he can come by whenever he wants, and you'll figure it out.*

They both sat and watched the movie while they ate popcorn and drank sodas. But the weight of the conversation hung over them the entire time. Neither of them could explain what the movie was about when it was over because they were too preoccupied, first with the reality that Vickie was a vampire and then, with what they would do next.

CHAPTER TWENTY-FIVE

The double-doors parted and Alexis and her father stepped into the big-box hardware store.

He put a brave face on for his daughter, walked through the turnstile at the front of the store, and pretended to try to get her stuck in it.

"Aren't you a little old for pranks like this, Dad?"

"You're never too old for a good prank, my dear. Follow me." He turned sharply right and walked into the blinding lights of the electrical department.

Row after row of overhead lights and ceiling fans beamed down on them. "Wow, look at all the choices. How come I've never been over here, Dad?"

"Because there are so many choices." He pointed to one ceiling fan that had a two-hundred-dollar price tag hung from its pull chain. "See what I mean? Besides, replacing a ceiling fan isn't something you do very often—or you shouldn't, anyway. That's why you haven't been here."

"After last night, I want to make sure I have the best one

possible." She was adamant about that point and her tone of voice clearly indicated that she was serious.

It was hard for him to blame his daughter and even he had to admit that her concerns were well-founded. Late the previous night, she had been in bed reading a book when she heard a *ping* sound. She looked up and the ceiling fan, which had been on medium speed, dislodged slowly from the bracket that attached it to the ceiling.

It fell directly above her, but the only reason it didn't actually plummet on top of her and break any of her bones was the electrical connection. It dangled from the wires and continued to spin in a violent nightmare.

She screamed, rolled off her bed, and army-crawled across her bedroom until she could reach the light switch to turn it off. Craig walked in to find her clutching her knees where she leaned against the wall while she stared in panic at the fan that dangled above her bed.

But, while he could readily understand, he tried to explain what had actually happened. "This was a faulty installation. It had nothing to do with the fan itself. We'll replace it and it will come with a new bracket we can install. It'll be a quick and easy fix, and you won't have to worry about that happening again."

"Who installed it?"

He shrugged. "Whoever built the house, I guess. It matches all the other ones. But, for whatever reason, that one was installed incorrectly. It was only a matter of time before something like this happened. But you have Super Dad here. I'll make sure the next one remains attached for a long time."

Alexis rolled her eyes at the Super Dad comment, but

she was also happy to see him in a somewhat better mood. Even if she could tell he was still a little sad, he tried to be happier. That was all she wanted from him.

"How do you think Vickie's doing on her date?" he asked his daughter.

"Who knows?" she responded sadly. "She's been really depressed lately. I only hope she can find her way out of it before it ruins her relationship with him."

"Do you think Eric will walk away?"

"Eh. It's not that. He's a sweet, supportive guy. But if she's going to be *Debbie Downer* on him all the time, I can't imagine he'll put up with that forever."

Her father glanced at the price tag of a small ceiling fan on the shelf. "Well, I'm proud of her. I know this is hard for her to handle, but she's done really well with fighting her instincts. I haven't heard of her using her powers at all."

"Yeah, but do you think that's healthy, Dad?" She admired a crystal-like light fixture hanging over her head. "I don't know how this works with vampires, but maybe it's bad that she can't use her powers. What if she physically needs to use them? Because if that is the case, this could be the first step towards her deterioration."

He turned to face her. "I know what you're saying. I'm trying to keep my eyes out for that. Here's the thing, though. Even if it's unhealthy for her to not use her powers, it's also really unhealthy for her to get caught using her powers. It's kind of a catch twenty-two situation here."

Alexis folded her arms and shook her head. "As much as it hurts me to say this, maybe it was a mistake to bring her here."

"I know. But by the same token, she was awake either way. Whether she does this here or she does this in Austria, she has to keep it under wraps. The Austrian government won't be any more welcoming to vampires than the American government. Either way, she has to hide. At least here, she has a support system in place that can work with her and help her."

The two of them wandered the aisles and examined various ceiling fans until they found a plain white one in a small box.

"And Bingo was his name-o!" Craig pulled the box off the shelf. "Here we go. Perfect for a small room."

"Dad, come on." She tried not to sound too whiny. "That's so plain. Can't we get one with a little style? It's so boring."

"It's also twenty dollars. We'll take this one. It's only a ceiling fan and it doesn't need to be anything fancy."

He spun the box to read the back. "Now, let me make sure it comes with the bracket, too. I've never actually done this before."

Disappointed, Alexis turned to face the wall of light bulbs and pull chains and noticed a tall, rather leggy blonde woman who appeared to be around her father's age. "Whoa, Dad!" she whispered and nudged him in the ribs.

"Not now, hon." He squinted while reading the side of the box.

"Dad!" She elbowed him again. "Check out the babe looking at light bulbs."

Annoyed, he looked up from the box and his gaze settled on a beautiful woman. *Yeah, but she probably doesn't look so good when she turns.* To his surprise, however, she was gorgeous. And that wasn't the only surprise.

"Holy cow, Craig Watson?" The woman's eyes widened and her mouth fell open into a stunned smile. "How are you?" She hurried up to him and embraced him in a warm hug.

"Hi, Katie!" He returned the hug. "I haven't seen you in ages."

"No kidding." She adjusted the strap on her purse over her shoulder. "Sheesh, it's probably been more than ten or fifteen years."

"Well, how have you been? What are you up to these days?"

"I'm in marketing for the Children's Hospital."

Of course. She always was so charitable. "Good for you. That sounds like the perfect job for you."

"It is. It's fun and I really like it. And who is this with you?"

Alexis waved. "Hi, I'm Alexis. I'm his daughter."

She shook her head in disbelief. "Craig, she's beautiful. High school?"

"Yeah, I'm a sophomore. For a few more weeks anyway."

"Jeez, Craig, do you remember when we were sopho-mores? That feels like a lifetime ago."

"I think it was." He tried to put on a good smile. She brought that out of him.

"Oh, and I'm so sorry to hear about your wife. I heard about that last year. How are you doing?" She touched him gently on the shoulder.

"Thanks. We're doing okay. We've been healing and

every day gets better, you know? At some point, you simply have to accept your lot in life and move forward. Besides, with this one at home, I have to keep my focus on the future."

"Gosh, well, I want to know more. Can I text you my number?"

Alexis raised her eyebrows. *Well, that one was straightforward enough. I thought he was worried about being alone?*

As she typed in her number, Craig couldn't help but look at her left hand. *No ring. After all these years, she has no ring.*

They exchanged numbers on their phones, then tucked them away with smiles on their faces. "Let's get together for coffee or dinner or something."

"I'd love that. I'll talk to you in a day or two and we'll set something up." He opened his arms and gave her another big hug.

"Thanks. And it was so nice to meet you, Alexis."

"You too."

"Talk soon." The woman walked away, and father and daughter watched her in silence for a moment.

"Dad, I don't want to be too weird, but what a babe. That woman was smoking hot and totally into you."

He smirked and passed the compliment off humbly. "Please. Katie? No."

"So you went to high school with her?" She took the ceiling fan box off the shelf.

"Yep. Katie Adam. And she's still single, I don't believe it."

Alexis stopped walking. "Wait—Katie Adam? Isn't that the yearbook girl?"

Her father nodded. Katie Adam had admitted on the last day of senior year that she had a crush on him by writing in his yearbook. He had a crush on her as well, but they never got together.

"Dad, this is meant to be."

"Didn't you tell me not so long ago that I needed to cool it and not put so much pressure on women? That was you, wasn't it?"

"Yeah, but this is kismet." She resumed walking, the box tucked under her arm. "You two always kinda-missed each other, and now you're both single? If you play your cards right, this will definitely go well."

"Alexis, I don't even know what cards I have anymore. And isn't this weird for you? We're talking about me dating someone who is not Mom." They reached the checkout line. "You're encouraging me to date around. That's weird."

"It's not weird, Dad. I'm rooting for you. I want you to be happy. And that means getting you companionship. That Katie girl looks like a knockout, and she seems really nice. If you have stuff in common, maybe you can find a nice little fit together."

Craig stuck his hands in his pockets as they stepped forward in line. "Katie's quite a babe. It would be fun to date her. But...don't forget your mom."

"How could I forget Mom?" The comment almost annoyed her. "Dad, Mom is gone. It's okay to date someone and it's okay for me to be excited about it for you. Besides, no woman will ever compare to Mom in the Babe Department anyway."

He laughed as they reached the register. "Your mom was definitely a babe."

She placed the box onto the counter. "She sure was, Dad. We'll not forget that, even if we do find someone awesome for you to be with."

"Thanks, sweetheart. I appreciate your support."

"It's my job. Now, let's get this thing home before another one falls on me."

Craig laughed while he inserted his debit card into the pay machine. "I don't even know what that means."

CHAPTER TWENTY-SIX

*A*ll right, Jim. Don't get too far ahead of yourself here. If *you are too eager and are too accusatory in this meeting, it's all over for you. Choose your words carefully.*

Trembo scanned his ID card to open the front door of the school. He turned right and immediately walked into Mr Goede's office.

"Good morning, Jim." The principal looked up from his desk as he jotted a few notes on the piece of music he was reviewing.

"Ned. What are you working on this morning?"

The man put the pencil down and tapped on the papers in front of him. "Oh, this is the quiet time of the day, so it's a good opportunity for me to go through new music to see if any of it would work for my choirs."

"The school year is almost over. Do you work that far in advance?"

He chuckled. "Jim, I know people say that educators have summers off, but I work year-round. I don't really have significantly more time in the summer, outside of a few planned trips and long weekends. I work constantly. If I come across new music, I try to review it as soon as possible." He closed the sheet music and set it aside. "Now, you're here first thing in the morning and you have come directly to my office. Obviously, you have something you want to discuss."

"I do." He sat in the chair closest to the desk. "I'd like to have a conversation with one of your students."

Mr Goede raised his eyebrows. "Okay. Are we concerned there is some evidence of performance-enhancing drugs?"

Remember, choose your words carefully. "I don't want to go that far. I merely saw some things that warranted a conversation. It's my first chance to talk to a student athlete here, and I think it's a good time to start having those conversations, as difficult as they may be."

With a nod, the principal opened his calendar. "Let's take a look at my agenda here. How soon do you want to meet this student? Today? I might be able to work something out, but I'd have to pull her out of class. Is it that important?"

"Well, it's very important, and enough so that I would pull a student out of a class. But do you really need to be there?"

The man sighed. "We went over this when I allowed you to come in, Jim. I'm fine with you investigating the school, but if this involves any of the students directly, I would like to be a part of it. I believe I can be an impartial voice of reason, depending on the situation and if it calls for it."

"Fine. Whatever works for you guys, then. I'm here all day."

"Which student do we need to meet with?" He placed his fingers on the keyboard, ready to punch in her name.

"Tracy Miller."

He looked surprised as he typed. "Tracy Miller is an excellent athlete and a very smart student. I'd be shocked if she were involved with any type of drugs."

This bias is why I don't want you in the meeting, Ned. Jeez. "I'm not accusing anyone of anything. I merely want to meet the girl and talk to her a little."

During the fourth hour of the day, the two men sat at a small conference table outside Mr Goede's office. As the bell rang in the halls, the athletic brunette stepped into the room. She wore a hooded sweatshirt that boasted of the girls' softball team's championship win from a season before, along with a pair of light gray sweatpants. Her hair was pulled up into a tight bun.

"You wanted to see me, Mr Goede?"

"Hi, Tracy." He smiled warmly at her. "Please have a seat. Do you recognize this gentleman?"

She sat, popped a bubble in her gum, and nodded. "Yeah, you're the new hall monitor."

He stood and extended his hand. "Jim Trembo. A pleasure to meet you, young lady."

"Am I in trouble?"

"No…" The principal tried to reassure her, then looked at him. "I don't believe so."

Jim sat decisively in his chair. "Tracy, you're not in trouble necessarily, but I wanted to ask you a few questions about your athletic abilities. It sounds to me like you are very involved in sports."

The girl slipped her backpack off and dropped it on the floor so she could be more comfortable. "Yeah. Cross country in the fall. Basketball in the winter. Track in the spring."

"That's a fairly full load." He produced a notebook and began to take notes. "And you're a junior?"

"Mmm-hmm."

"Now, hang on a second. You said you run track but you're wearing a softball shirt."

She laughed. "Yeah, my friend Kristi is on the team. I borrowed it once and haven't given it back yet."

What is with all these girls and trading clothes? When I was in high school, guys didn't trade clothes like this all the time. He scribbled a few more notes. "Tracy, do you own a pink Clear Lake High School Cross Country Team sweatshirt?"

Confused, she looked at Mr Goede, who also seemed befuddled by the question. "Yeah, I do."

"Okay." He wrote something else. "Do you have it with you? Maybe in your locker or something?"

"No. I keep it at home if I'm not wearing it."

The principal leaned forward. "What exactly does this have to do with drug use?"

"Trust me. I know what I'm doing." He turned to the girl. "I was at the track meet over the weekend. I saw you take a spill during the three thousand two hundred."

Her face burned bright red. "Ugh. I don't know if that was more infuriating or embarrassing. I would have won that race if I hadn't fallen."

"Here's the thing, though, Tracy. You took a rather

devastating fall. I was there. I winced when it happened because it looked so painful."

She shrugged. "It hurt a little. What's your point?"

"My point is, you took a nasty fall, got up, and continued running. How is that possible?"

"It's very possible. You don't stop until the race is over, sir. I didn't think twice about it. I pushed through the pain."

"But…even though you fell, you don't have a mark on you from it, do you?"

Tracy ran her fingers up into her sleeve and over the arm she had fallen on. "No, I was lucky, I guess."

He smirked. "Sure. Lucky."

Mr Goede raised a finger. "Tracy, dear, can you wait out in the hall for a quick minute while I convene with Mr. Trembo? It won't be long and you can come back in. Thank you!" He closed the door behind her and spun to face Jim. "What on Earth are you trying to do?"

"What?" Jim was genuinely confused by the question.

"You're investigating this poor girl because she fell? Are you insane?"

Carefully. Make it up as you go. "There are certain performance-enhancing drugs that aid with rapid healing. Now, none of them have proven to be the magic bullet that keeps you from getting hurt, but it can get you back on your feet again quickly. She could have that stuff in her veins. We simply don't know."

The principal's face was so red, it was almost purple. "Well, I know. I know that Tracy Miller is a model student and an excellent representative of our school at any public event. She is clean, and it is utterly strange to me that you base this accusation on an observation that, honestly, could be mistaken. Maybe she didn't fall hard enough to leave a mark. I don't know. But if you think you can simply march in here and accuse my star students of cheating, you'd better be really sure they are."

He opened the door and welcomed Tracy into the room once again. She was wary of Trembo now but maintained a brave face in spite of the intimidation.

"Tracy, I didn't mean to accuse you of anything. I apologize because that was not the point of this meeting."

"Thank you."

"I was simply…concerned for your well-being. The way you fell looked like you had been seriously injured, and I was as relieved as anyone else watching that you were able to get up from that completely unscathed."

She nodded. "Okay. So are we done here?"

Jim leaned forward and looked deeply into her eyes in an attempt to see beyond whatever mask she might have put in place. "Have you ever resorted to taking…unfair advantages to win races and other sporting events?"

The term unfair advantages was the best cover description he could come up with. He did not want the conversation to be about drugs. It had to be about super-powers. But with Mr Goede sitting beside him, he had to make it seem like he was talking about performance-enhancing drugs.

To his frustration, he could tell from the look in Tracy's eyes that she was telling the truth. She hadn't taken any shortcuts.

"Sir, with all due respect, steroids are stupid," Tracy said firmly. "All that stuff—it's stupid. The drugs wind up getting all the credit. I'd rather win a race because I worked harder and was legitimately faster than the other runner instead of winning a race because I took a pill."

"So you never have?"

"No way. I've run since I was four years old. I win races on my own. If I took drugs to try to win, I'd probably win every race for a really long time."

After she had been excused, the principal stared at Trembo, his expression openly skeptical. "That didn't go well."

Jim shrugged. "We achieved what we needed to achieve with her. I'll find another way to discover where this is all coming from."

Mr Goede sighed. "I need to get back to my office. I'm not sure how I feel about all this, to be honest. You need to do far better. I am ready to end this entire exercise if you can't maintain decorum. These kids are safe here. Don't use them to advance a cause at the expense of their trust because you get to leave this place when you're done. I have to clean the mess you leave behind you with your roughshod behavior."

"Yes, sir."

The man walked out and Jim shook his head. *Maybe that would have gone better if he didn't insist on sitting there the whole time. Regardless, she definitely told the truth. I need to find a better way to weed this kid out.*

CHAPTER TWENTY-SEVEN

Behind the curtain in the Clear Lake High School auditorium, Vickie peeked out to see all the students filing in. *Holy cow, there are so many of them. How am I supposed to talk in front of so many people? And why does this scare me? My stomach is going crazy.*

"Are you nervous?" Emily grinned at her when she turned.

"Yes. But why?" She shook her head in confusion. "I'm not in mortal danger. I'm not, like, going to be physically hurt out there. The worst that can happen is I say the wrong thing. That's not so bad, is it?"

Adam Thiele stood in the background, picked at his fingernails, and smirked. "You've never spoken in public before?" She shook her head. "It reminds me of a Jerry Seinfeld joke. He said, 'Studies show that public speaking is the number one fear of most people. Number two is death. That means that, if you were attending a funeral, you'd rather be in the casket than doing the eulogy.'"

He laughed at the joke but Vickie only smiled politely. The other two chuckled.

"It's true." Emily nodded. "Public speaking can be scary. You're simply worried about being embarrassed. But you know your stuff. I'm sure it'll be fine."

The vampire felt good about her memory. Her advanced memorization skills helped that along. Once she had cobbled together what she wanted to say, all she had to do was read it a couple of times and it was ingrained in her mind. But for some reason, she still wasn't very confident.

It wasn't as though the previous few weeks had helped her feel confident. Her team struggled to get through the project.

Adam spent every get-together in exactly the same way —his feet up, no books, no notes, picked at his fingernails, and generally ignored everyone. He did zero work and he did not come prepared at all.

As a result, the rest of the group had to take up his slack. Sam took direction well enough, but he always needed to be told what to do next. This made it very distracting whenever anyone tried to get their own section of the work done.

As for Emily, she seemed to be a smart and capable group member. She helped work on a little of the presentation and largely took care of the multimedia aspect of it— the images and slides that would be presented. Of course, both Sam and she had to talk, but they'd managed to keep their part to a minimum.

To Vickie's dread, the group followed through with their assumption that she would lead the entire presentation. She had note cards in front of her that she didn't really need, but she wanted to look like an average student. And even though she was ready, she still literally shook with terror.

"You aren't going to pass out up there, are ya?" Adam laughed at her. "Keep it together. If you blow it in front of the whole school, you'll never hear the end of it."

"Yeah, right, Adam. You'd probably be the first person to make fun of her," Sam chimed in as he tried his best to buddy up with the cool kid.

She felt so awkward. *I've never been this nervous and not felt my fangs come in or the urge to run or any of that. My powers aren't queued up, but I'm still unable to sit still here. This is the strangest thing.*

"Welcome to this year's health assembly." Ms Marozick spoke into a microphone behind the podium on stage. "Now, we do ask that the entire student body is on their best behavior for these presentations. You are all being monitored by the faculty seated among you, and your behavior will be graded accordingly, along with the students here. Please respect the hard work they put in."

From behind the curtain, Adam couldn't help but continue his snark. "Yeah," he whispered. "Respect my hard work."

Vickie gritted her teeth, ready to punch him. The other two laughed at the harmless humor, even though they'd had to do more work to pick up his slack.

The vampire couldn't quite make sense out of it. *Why are they even buddying up to him in the first place? Because he makes them laugh sometimes? He's also a huge jerk who added work to our plate and will get a good grade without doing anything. This is so stupid.*

If there was one aspect of American culture that she had trouble fully understanding, it was the concept of the class clown. To her, education was a serious pursuit and something that required a respectful attitude. Yet, in the majority of her classes, there were kids—usually boys— who joked constantly throughout class, distracted other kids, and failed grades.

Adam fell into that category, and it made her want to scream. Fortunately for his safety, they were about to head onstage.

Emily smiled and waved at the crowd as they applauded the group's entrance. She situated herself at the projector, ready to move the slides forward. Vickie walked cautiously up to the podium and adjusted the microphone to her height.

As she pulled on it, a squeal emitted from the speakers. Her stomach lurched and her fangs poked her tongue ever so slightly. The audience groaned and a murmur rippled through the students.

"Sorry," she said loudly into the microphone. "Good afternoon, everyone." With a shaky voice, she started her presentation.

"We were tasked with the health benefits of a regular running or jogging practice. Studies have shown that regular cardiovascular exercise is a leading factor in the longevity of your life."

As she spoke, Emily followed efficiently and moved the slides to display graphs and other statistics about jogging and running.

The vampire continued, although she made the mistake of looking at a few of the students. She saw Alexis, who smiled encouragingly at her. This filled her with a renewed sense of confidence. It helped to know that she had a friend out there.

But that confidence soon dissipated when she saw many of the goof-off students literally falling asleep in their seats.

"Um…so, running has been a part of human history. In fact, long-distance running, in particular, has been shown to be a crucial part of our human abilities. It is the only ability we have that animals do not have. This is how we survived as a species in the early days of man. If someone needed to hunt but did not have weapons, he could pursue an animal until it collapsed from exhaustion. The same is true if the roles were reversed. As long as man could stay a touch faster than the other animals, he could survive. But how do you do that today? I don't think any of us will try to outrun a cheetah, and you don't have to chase a pizza until it dies from exhaustion."

Vickie was proud of that joke. She thought it was funny, but the line was met with silence from the student body. Her amused smile transformed almost immediately into an embarrassed smile. The blood rushed to her face and tears filled her eyes.

You're bombing out here. This is not going well at all. You don't have their interest at all. You'll totally fail this class and the group will be furious with you as well.

After a longer than comfortable pause, she tried to speak, but she had lost her place in her note cards because she hadn't actually used them. "Um…and, uh…running is… Well, it doesn't have to be difficult…"

She felt like she couldn't even breathe. It was suffocating, and the entire school now watched it unfold. Vickie sweated and breathed heavily, in a state close to panic.

Unexpectedly, Adam stood calmly from his chair behind her, gave her a nudge, and pulled the microphone up to his level. "Thanks for starting us off strong, Vickie. All right, guys, here's the deal—running is not only good for you, it's easy."

To her astonishment, he had taken the presentation over when his responsibility had simply been a few closing lines. She took a few steps back to let him do whatever it was he attempted to do.

He snatched the microphone off the stand and held it in his hands as he stepped away from the podium. "If you hate running or think you can't do it, that's because you're working off other people's expectations. Knock it off." The crowd chuckled. "Vickie's right. It's hard to run when you aren't trying to survive. But that's the thing—you are trying to survive. You're not outrunning a saber-toothed tiger. You're outrunning heart disease, cancer, cardiovascular illnesses, and obesity. Do you want to not be fat for the rest of your life? Get outside and pound the pavement."

A few whoops and cheers rang out of the crowd from his buddies. "And let's go further than that. Many people say they're bad at running. Folks, no one's bad at running. Can you walk? Then you can walk faster. That's running. You merely can't keep up with other people. Cool. The only person you have to beat is yourself."

Vickie marveled at his confidence. He didn't merely deliver it with an attractive personality, but he was also covered all the materials they had gone over as a group.

"If you've never run a day in your life, start walking.

Then run from the end of one driveway to the end of another one. The next day, maybe you run two driveways. Or you run one again. I don't care. The key is to always push yourself a little farther. Work up a sweat. Very soon, you'll put up miles almost as often as Vickie does."

She smiled nervously. The crowd was engaged and awake.

"And here's the most important reason why running should be a part of your life, guys. It's free. There are no gym memberships and no equipment to buy. You can run barefoot if you want—people do it all the time. No trails or roads will charge you to run on them…except probably the ones in Illinois. You'd have to get a City Pass to run on their roads."

The crowd erupted at the dig at Illinois.

At the end of the presentation, once Emily and Sam had added their small contribution, everyone smiled. The student body applauded eagerly. Adam had completely saved the day and nailed it down.

By the time they returned to behind the curtain, the vampire was in shock. Everyone high-fived and Adam exuded cool confidence. He had been prepared the whole time in case he was needed.

Ms Marozick ducked back and was ecstatic. "You guys were a fantastic team. Oh, you caught all the science and all the practical reasons why running makes sense as a foundation for your health. I normally don't give the grades out right away, but you will all get A's for this one. Well done."

Vickie was relieved and exhaled deeply. She looked at Adam in shock and he gave her a confident wink.

She turned to walk out into the hallway and saw Alexis

waiting for her with a big hug. "Adam really saved your butt out there."

"He did. I don't even know how to thank him. I wasn't expecting that at all."

Her sister giggled. "Sometimes, people can surprise you. But hey, you're out of the woods now. It's over. And no one got hurt."

"Not this time, anyway. I never want to do that again." She headed to the bubbler to get a drink of water, relieved that she could finally relax—about that, anyway.

CHAPTER TWENTY-EIGHT

"My parents will seriously kill me." Eric tried to ease the car door closed after he parked it on the street in front of the Watson house.

Vickie waited for him on the front porch. "How was the drive?"

"Terrifying."

He had only recently obtained his temporary license and legally, he could not drive without an adult in the car with him. Normally, he'd have abided by that, but Vickie had urged him to find a way to get to her house that night and he'd finally succumbed to temptation.

They greeted each other with a kiss. "Your group crushed the presentation today. Nice work."

"Was it obvious that I was nervous?"

He laughed. "Is it obvious that I'm nervous?" He looked around and up and down the street as if someone waited to bust him.

"This neighborhood is full of people who are out at all times of the night on the street, okay?" She took him by the hand. "As long as your parents stay asleep, you won't get in any trouble."

"What about Alexis or her dad?"

"Trust me. They'll be fine."

The full moon hung in the sky above their heads and at any other time, romance would have been the first thing on his mind. Now, however, his thoughts were waylaid by larger issues. *What am I thinking? This is crazy. Suicide. Absolute insanity.* Only half an hour before, he'd locked the door to his bedroom and slipped out the window with the keys to his parents' car. He had never driven so carefully before, paranoid that he would be pulled over and in a heap of trouble.

But he loved his girl. And once she told him she was a vampire, he honestly had no clue what to expect anymore.

He didn't, however, expect her to be in an old-fashioned gown. "What are you wearing?"

She tugged at the old fabric. "This is what I wore for four hundred years. It's a gown I was dressed in when my parents put me to sleep in a coffin in our house. I keep it because wearing it connects me to the old days—my family and my history. In it, I still feel like a vampire."

She's losing her mind. Will I be seriously injured here? I still have my phone in my pocket in case I need to call the police, right?

"I know you like to follow the rules. I do too." She led him to the back yard. "I know that this all scares you."

"Right, but now that you say you're a vampire, I definitely won't argue with you," he teased.

"Why, because you're worried that I'll suck your blood?"

"No, because I worry that you've lost your grip on reality." He scoffed but stopped himself quickly. "Vickie, I know there has been any number of weird things that have happened lately, and I can't quite explain it all either, but it worries me that you think you're a vampire."

She stopped him on the far side of the shed, concealed from the house. "That's why you're here. I know you don't believe me. You've made that clear. But I need to prove this to you. All you have to do is stand here and wait. Watch—keep your eyes on that first tree directly ahead from here."

Eric squinted to locate the one she meant. They were lucky that it was a clear night and the full moon illuminated the field and the trees on the far side. He looked at the one at the front of the line at the edge of the forest. "Okay, what am I looking for?"

Vickie smiled. "Me."

Before he could respond, she bolted to the tree hundreds of yards away. Her white gown glowed brightly enough that he could see her.

His stomach dropped. He froze in place, unable to comprehend the evidence of his eyes. All he could do was shake his head in disbelief.

With another quick sprint, she appeared directly in front of him. The suddenness of her appearance knocked him off his feet. "Jeez!" He flailed his arms as he fell onto the grass.

The vampire laughed and extended her hand to help him up. He hesitated to take it. "It's okay. I'm still me. Let me help you." Once she'd hauled him to his feet, she held both his hands. "This is who I am, Eric. I am a vampire. It doesn't mean I will ever hurt you. Ever. I have full control over my powers. I will never use those powers to do anything that might harm you or put you in danger."

He held his breath and remained silent because he didn't know what to think. After a moment, he took a few steps away from her and looked at the tree, then back at his girlfriend. She smiled at him to reveal long fangs.

"Should I be scared of those?" He pointed nervously.

She touched the tips of them with her tongue and giggled. "No. I don't eat human flesh. I don't suck blood. Remember, Sangs do that, not vampires."

"Are there...more of you?" He held the back of his head while his rampant thoughts still tried to make sense of all this.

"From everything that I have known and seen, I am the last vampire." She folded her hands and stepped forward. "Sangs are a different story. Do you remember Alexis's ex-boyfriend, Will?"

"Ugh. That guy was a creeper."

"Right. Because he's a Sang."

Eric blinked a few times. "What? So Will feasts on human flesh?"

Vickie's tone became matter of fact. "Actually, Will and I were mortal enemies for a while. We had some huge, bloody fights but somehow, I got through to him that we needed to watch each other's backs."

"What happened? Where is he? He disappeared off the face of the earth."

"Yeah. I don't know where he is either, but I can sense that he's not anywhere near here. I was hunted by an ancient cult called the Circle. They wanted to rid the world of vampires, so they came here and tried to kill me out there in the field."

"I can't even...how am I supposed to process all this information?" He paced feverishly as he struggled to take it all in.

"Anyway, they had me dead to rights out there. I thought I was a goner but Will arrived out of nowhere and obliterated them. He dragged their bodies into the woods and I never saw them—or him—again."

Eric twisted his face in disgust. "That's horrible."

"I know. But they were also three grown men who tried to murder a teenage girl, so who's the worst there?"

He smiled. "You're not a teenager. You're four hundred years old."

She laughed, relieved that he could make a joke, even a small one. "Okay, technically..." She threw her arms around his neck and kissed him. "You're not scared of me?"

"Oh, I'm terrified. Absolutely terrified." They both laughed. "But you have been honest with me. And you say that you won't hurt me."

"Nope. I won't."

"Then I'm all yours." He stepped away from her. "So... what else can you do?"

Vickie giggled again and proceeded to explain to her boyfriend about her heightened senses and her ability to sense danger. "And super-strength, too. When I'm really going, I can lift almost anything."

"Such as?"

"What, I have to prove that to you too?"

"Vickie, I'm out here at 2:00 am after driving illegally

across town. The least you can do is pick something up. I want the full show here."

Ah, he's right about that. She darted into the woods and returned with a log that was three times her size. While she held it over her head with one hand and raised and lowered it, she pretended to yawn.

He laughed at the show. "You look like a cartoon character. Okay, I believe you. Go put it back before you get caught."

Soon, the two of them sat in the grass behind the shed. Her head was on his shoulder and they stared at the moon.

"This is actually awesome," he admitted.

"I thought for sure you would be scared away."

"I almost was. But I've trusted you this whole time so there's no reason to stop trusting you now. I'm a little scared, though."

Vickie stroked his hand. "Of what?"

"You said there was a group that tried to kill you. And they got close. What happens if another group comes after you? If Will's not around to save you and they know how to kill you, are you simply out of luck?"

"I don't know." She sighed and looked at the moon again. "I can't guarantee anything. I know that something is going on."

"What do you mean?"

She proceeded to explain to him the feelings she'd had, the stomach pains, and the waves of panic that washed over her from time to time.

"And you don't know what any of it means?"

"Not really. I know it means something worse than the

Circle, but I don't really know if it's another group, a monster, a person, or what."

He squeezed her tightly. "I don't want anything to happen to you."

"I don't want anything to happen to you either."

They stood from the grass when they decided 3:00 am was a good enough time for Eric to get back home. "I really hope my parents don't know I'm gone. But it was worth it." He kissed her, and the two of them walked up the driveway to his car.

"Does this change how we date?" He stopped at the car and put his hands on her waist. "I mean, do I have to alter my dating strategy now that you're a vampire?"

She rolled her eyes. "Hey, dummy, I've always been a vampire. It's not broke. Don't try to fix it. We have something good going here."

"Yeah, we do." He kissed her again. "I'm glad to have some of this awkwardness behind us."

"The last few weeks haven't been the most fun." She shook her head. "I'm sorry. I simply didn't know how to handle it."

"It's okay. I understand why now. But promise me you'll be honest with me in the future."

Vickie laughed and ran her fingers through the hair on the back of his head. "If this didn't scare you off for good, I have nothing else to hide."

"I hope not." They shared one more kiss before he climbed into the car and drove nervously down the road to head home.

She looked at the moon and smiled. *I'm so glad that's over with. And we're still together. No more secrets from him.*

Then, she thought of something. She walked to the front porch where her phone was, picked it up, and opened a text to Eric.

Shoot me a text when you get home so I know you made it safely. Good luck with your parents! Love you.

CHAPTER TWENTY-NINE

Pete Stabone walked into his hotel room carrying a plastic bag from a trip to the mall across the street. He sighed loudly to himself and groaned at the unavoidable reality that he still had to look at the inside of his hotel room.

He'd barely dropped the bag onto the spare bed and kicked his shoes off when his phone buzzed. With a grimace, he located the remote and turned on ESPN for background noise to keep him company while he pulled his phone out and checked his messages.

Pete, meet me down in the bar in 10 minutes

"Man, I hope this is good news." He rolled his eyes and shoved his feet into his shoes, turned the TV off, and walked out into the hallway.

When he reached the hotel bar, Jim waited for him with a drink in his hand. He walked up behind him and sat on a stool. "Will this take long? I'm not really in the mood to have a drink tonight."

The other man smiled at him and patted him on the

shoulder. "You don't have time to have a drink tonight, Pete."

He frowned as he considered what this might mean. "What are you talking about?"

With a knowing smile, his boss fumbled in the inside pocket of his suit jacket and withdrew a piece of paper, which he thumped onto the bar in front of him.

Pete leaned over and read the ticket. "This is a ticket to Ronald Reagan International Airport, Jim." He looked at his colleague in confusion and disbelief.

"Your flight leaves in about two and a half hours, my friend. That should be enough time for you to pack and take an Uber to Mitchell International." He smiled and took a sip of his drink.

"Are you serious right now? Don't dangle this carrot in front of me if you simply intend to take it away." He clutched the airplane ticket in his hands.

"It's been a long trip. Go home, Pete. I already sent the other guys home on flights. They've all left."

Pete laughed with utter relief at finally being released to go see his wife and kids. "I can't wait to call her. She'll totally lose her mind!" Then, his smile dropped. "Wait, what does this mean for the investigation? It's not over yet."

Jim shook his head. "No, it's not. But this portion of it is for now. I've obtained everything I can out of what we have here in Milwaukee."

"Are you quitting? You're not flying back to DC, are you?"

"I'm not quitting. I merely have to continue the

research." He seemed somewhat disappointed to go back out on the road and away from Milwaukee.

"But you're so close. We know this supernatural being is here in Milwaukee. We also know that it's at Clear Lake High School. You can't get any closer than this."

His boss sniffed. "Yeah, but unless I can interview every last student in Clear Lake High School without tipping off any suspicions, I need more information before I can move forward. And I definitely won't find that information here in Milwaukee—not in the field and not at the school."

Pete shook his head. "Then where will you go?"

With another devilish smile, Jim placed another plane ticket on the bar top.

Leaning forward, Pete read that one out loud as well. "Salzburg Airport WA Mozart? You're going to Austria?"

Jim nodded confidently. "I leave first thing in the morning. I have one more night to enjoy the Wisconsin hospitality." With that, he nodded at the bartender and gestured with his drink to order one more.

"Do you have a lead out there?"

"We know this creature comes from Austria because of the history of the sword we found. The weapon belonged to the Circle—a group of vampire hunters, basically. And they were based in Austria."

Pete ran his fingers through his thinning hair. "Right, but the Circle existed hundreds of years ago. It's not like they have a headquarters or anything anymore."

"Actually, I've done a little reading." The bartender placed a fresh drink in front of him. "Thanks, buddy. I have found documentation that the Circle still exists and is actively meeting in Austria. They tried to hunt this girl once already, so there must be people there who know the info they were working from."

His colleague rested his elbow on the bar and propped his head on his hand. "So let me get this straight...you're literally inches away from finding this creature and validating your entire career, potentially changing the American military as we know it. Everything you've spent decades pursuing is within your grasp and now, you have to fly to the other side of the hemisphere so you can get directions?"

Jim uttered a belly laugh. "I wouldn't exactly word it that way, but yeah, that's exactly what I'm doing. What do you think?"

"I think it's insanity!" He had raised his voice to the point where other patrons of the bar had begun to look at them.

"Pete, you're starting to attract attention. Dial it down."

"You are so close. This is stupid and a waste of money."

He didn't lose his confident smile. "Think of it like this. I could spend six months or more investigating the school to try to locate this being. Or I could fly to Austria, talk to the Circle, find out who this is, and be back within a week to apprehend it. I'll save loads of time by doing it this way."

"I don't know, Jim." Pete stared at the mirror behind the bar as he had so often when he'd sat there over the past few months. "It's weird. Seriously, this isn't the Middle Ages— not that they had airplanes then, but that's not the point. We have cell phones. Can't you call someone?"

"Do you think ancient Austrian religious sects have a listing in the Yellow Pages?" He laughed. "All I know is where and when they meet. That's all I have to work with, and that's all I need. I'll head there and meet them in person. Besides, then I can prove that I'm serious." His companion didn't reply, so the silence hung in the air for a second. "Pete, get back to your room and pack your bags. You gotta get to the airport, my friend."

He smiled and instantly forgot about the perceived insanity of Jim's plan. Hastily, he slid off the stool and snatched the plane ticket up. "Thanks, Jim. Good luck. Are you sure you're okay with this on your own?"

Jim lifted his glass. "I'll call you if I need you, Pete. Go home."

Pete laughed. "I'm going home."

———

The next morning, Jim Trembo walked through Mitchell International Airport and dragged his rolling suitcase behind him. He stopped at his gate and pulled his ticket out.

Let's see... Milwaukee to Toronto to Frankfurt to Salzburg. Well, no one said the job was easy. Three flights there, three flights back, which makes about fourteen hours of travel time. I'd better get comfortable.

After a day of connecting flights, different airports, and checking into one of the smallest hotels he'd ever stayed in, he was on a bus traveling into the town of Salzburg.

He breathed the fresh air coming off the water as he exited and smiled at his good fortune. *Even though this whole thing is a tremendous pain in the butt, I get to at least enjoy the cultures around the world. That's the best part.*

The Hohensalzburg Fortress loomed above, and he

made a note to himself that he wanted to explore that in the morning. But the sun was setting on his first day in Salzburg and he knew there would be a meeting held that evening.

After consulting his map, Jim made his way to the street outside a small cathedral. He tried his best to blend in with the tourists and other people who milled about and walked casually up the steps and through the large wooden doors that formed the entrance to the building.

Once the door closed behind him, the hustle and bustle of the outside world disappeared. In its place was a solemn silence, a respectful hum of quiet worship conducted by various people who had come to the cathedral. He watched some light candles for loved ones. Others knelt in pews and stared at the large images of Christ.

For a moment, he paused in the chapel area and studied the beautiful architecture and craftsmanship displayed throughout the building. He heard the noise of the street sneak its way into the building for a moment.

When he turned, a man walked in and closed the door behind him, carrying some kind of cloth on his shoulder. He looked at Trembo and nodded politely.

Curious, Jim watched the man duck under a velvet rope that blocked off the stairway and rush down to the basement of the church. *That's it. That's where they'll meet. I'm in the right place after all.*

Moving quietly so he would not disturb anyone or be detected, he ducked under the velvet rope and tiptoed down the steps and into the pitch-black darkness below.

When he finally reached the bottom of the steps, he

paused and stared at the glow of the candles that danced all over the walls of the underground area.

"Fellow Members of the Circle, we gather here today to once again honor the memory and ministry of our dear departed members, who succumbed to the evil that still ravages this planet. While today we mourn, we know that one will come who will help to bring this evil to its knees and finally eliminate it from the world once and for all. Humanity's future depends on it, and while we do not know the day or time when we will be saved from the torturous existence of the vampire race, we do believe and trust that we will see the day when it will be cleansed from the surface of the earth once and for all."

A smile spread across Jim's face as he stepped forward.

"For today, the Circle has been weakened. But tomorrow is a new day. We will rise from the ashes stronger than ever and more resolved to fight the good fight to restore peace and safety—and honor—to the great society of human beings currently in the shadow of the evil vampires."

He cleared his throat audibly. A gasp rushed through the small group as they turned toward him.

Showtime.

CHAPTER THIRTY

On that same day, Vickie called a family meeting.

Amused, Craig walked into the room. "I thought I was the only one who called family meetings. This is bogus. Who made you the dad?"

Vickie smiled in response. "It's not a Dad Meeting, it's a Family Meeting. By definition, any member of the family can call one, right?"

Alexis groaned as she walked into the kitchen. "They can, but they don't. The only ones who ever want a family meeting are the parents. You're doing this backward."

"Sit down, please."

Everyone took their place around the table. Craig folded his hands in front of him. "Okay, boss, what's on the agenda for the meeting today?"

"Guys, Eric's coming over for dinner tonight."

Father and daughter looked at each other, confused. "So?" Alexis spoke first. "This is worth a meeting?"

Craig pointed to his daughter. "I'm with her but that's fine. I wish you had asked ahead of time, but I'm making meatloaf tonight. That can stretch to another mouth. As long as we can save some leftovers."

"That's not why I called the meeting." She closed her eyes and took a deep breath. "I told Eric."

The air seemed to suck out of the room. He pursed his lips. "You told Eric what?"

She stared at him and didn't have to say it.

"Aw, crap!" He scowled. "Are you serious right now? Tell me you're only asking for permission to tell him."

"I told him. I even had him over here and demonstrated my powers to him. He knows everything."

He rubbed his temples. "Are you crazy? We're only now reaching a point where everything is under control and you're not attracting that much attention. We're finally in a good place here where I feel like we've found a routine. And you told him? What were you thinking?"

"Look, I only—"

"Do you think you're going to marry him? I know things worked differently where you're from. But here in America, most people don't marry their high school sweethearts. I thought we talked about this."

"I wanted to—"

"And what if he starts to tell other people? If it comes up casually in conversation, your cover is blown completely. This is exactly the opposite of what we've tried to do here, Vickie. You've introduced a new variable into this equation and it could result in word getting out about you."

"Hey!" Alexis slapped the top of the table with her palm and jolted everyone into silence. "Now, I agree with Dad, but can we at least give Vickie a chance to explain herself before we run her down like that?"

Craig's anger subsided a little. "You're right. I'm sorry, Vickie. Please explain why you decided to do this."

"Thank you." Calmly, she explained how Eric had become focused on the video and he knew something was suspicious. She said that he would have worked it out for himself.

"She's right there, Dad," her sister confirmed. "He cornered me about the video too. Of anyone I ever talked to about that video, he was the most obsessed with it. He knew something was wrong."

"Girls, I like Eric. But can he be trusted with this information? Or are we opening up an entirely new can of worms here?"

"I trust Eric. If I didn't, I wouldn't have told him."

Alexis nodded. "Yeah, I agree there. Eric's a good guy. There's no chance that he will tell anyone about this. I can vouch for his character. If that's the main concern here, we have nothing to worry about. He won't tell a soul."

About an hour later, Eric sat at the table for dinner with Vickie and the Watsons. He smiled when he saw the spread. "Whew. Meatloaf, mashed potatoes, and steamed broccoli. These are, like, my favorite foods. Did you plan it like this?"

Craig lifted a mouthful of meatloaf to his lips. "We don't think about you that much, Eric." He winked at him with a chuckle so he knew he was kidding. As he chewed, he continued to talk. "But...there's something we do need to talk about, young man."

He craned his neck and prepared himself for the worst,

even though he had absolutely no idea what the worst would prove to be.

"Vickie tells us she revealed some things to you recently. Very secret things."

"Yes, sir." He nodded. "I'm aware of how serious it is. I won't tell a soul about it."

Alexis laughed. "That's exactly what I said."

Her father did not laugh, however. "I know you're a good guy. But we're trusting you with this. If word gets out about her and what she is, she could be put in incredible danger. You are part of a very exclusive circle of trust here, limited to the people around this table. Do not take that lightly. This isn't some silly little high school secret. Her safety depends on it being kept under wraps."

"I understand, sir. Completely. It doesn't leave this room."

He nodded. "Good." He stuck his fork into his mashed potatoes and loaded it with a generous mouthful. "So, when is the wedding?"

Eric's eyes widened. "Excuse me?"

Craig didn't back down and kept his expression solemn. "The wedding. Now that you know her biggest secret, you'll have to marry her. Do you want to have a family ceremony or simply go to Vegas and elope or something?" He burst out laughing when he saw how nervous Eric had become. "Relax, kid. I'm only giving you a hard time."

Everyone laughed and the tension finally left the room.

The meal was enjoyable. Everyone joked and talked, and the dinner felt idyllic for all those involved.

Finally, things were starting to sort themselves out.

Vickie had a loving boyfriend whom she kept no secrets from, and she had control over her powers.

Alexis had a great boyfriend as well, with a budding relationship heading into the summer.

Craig had another chance to woo a woman he had a long history with.

Things were falling into place for the first time in years.

Once they were done eating, Eric pointed to the leftovers. "Would you mind if I take any of this home?I'm a huge fan of cold meatloaf sandwiches and I never pass up an opportunity to grab some. You can say no if you want."

Craig laughed at the suggestion. "I'll send you two slices, but that's it. I like leftovers, too, you know."

"No problem. Thank you."

He nodded in response, then turned to Vickie. "Hey, I have a cheesecake in the fridge. Do you want to pull that out with some plates, please?"

"Sure." She stood from the table and headed to the fridge.

Alexis gave her dad an impressed look. "You made cheesecake today?"

He shrugged. "I was in a dessert mood. Why not?"

"I'm not arguing. I'm only surprised."

Vickie carried the cheesecake in the glass pan across the kitchen floor. "This smells amazing. I can't wait to—" Before she could finish the sentence, she doubled over and the pan fell from her hands.

It shattered on the floor and cheesecake and cherry filling splattered the walls and the linoleum.

The vampire stumbled and fell onto her back, clutching her stomach, and Craig leapt from his chair and put his hand behind her neck. "What's going on, dear? Vickie, what is it?"

She groaned as sweat poured from her forehead. In her mind, she saw a man descending a staircase into darkness, surrounded by flames.

"Something's happening," she screamed.

"Oh, no," Alexis muttered.

"What's going on?" Eric asked her, freaked out.

"Vickie has had a sense that something terrible was coming—worse than the Circle. It's gradually got more intense in the past few weeks, but she kept trying to ignore it, though. It doesn't look like she can ignore it any longer."

Vickie moaned and sobbed on the floor. She managed to catch her breath but was still in a great deal of pain. She looked at Craig. "This is bad. This is so bad."

"I thought you said this already."

"But nothing happened. I can see it now. I can see something happening. Forces are coming together, and they will not stop until I'm dead or under their control."

"Vickie, will you be okay?" Eric knelt beside her.

She looked at him with a sense of pity. "I'm sorry that I brought you into this. A war is about to start. And I don't know how it'll end."

The Agency realized they were tracking the wrong girl and their sites are on Vickie. Does she have enough allies to help protect her from The Agency? Don't miss the exciting conclusion to The Last Vampire series with The Triumphant Girl!

Get sneak peeks, exclusive giveaways, behind the scenes content, and more.
PLUS you'll be notified of special **one day only fan pricing** on new releases.

Sign up today to get free stories.

CLICK HERE

or visit: https://marthacarr.com/read-free-stories/

I've lived here a year now and have settled into the place. Everything about this dream house has had a little magic attached to it. It started from the first day with the way I found it. I was a couple miles away at another subdivision late on a Sunday with my friend, Sheila, the realtor. The houses we were looking at were okay, but nothing special. I knew there was a fancier subdivision just those two little miles away. Why not go look at the model homes for fun?

We got there just before they were all closing and as we walked up the sidewalk, Sheila pointed out that the driveway had already been converted. This builder was itching to leave and be done. We went inside the largest house, oohing and aahing at all the upgrades, following around another couple and telling them, "You should buy it!"

We stopped to make small talk with the saleswoman who spoke in such a thick Eastern European accent, we could barely understand her. But she got across that there was just one house left and as she rattled off the specifics of the house Sheila started elbowing me. "It's like they heard you!" she whispered. Everything I wanted right down to a bay window in the master bedroom. On a whim we made a very lowball offer and I thought that would be the end of it.

Three days later they took my offer and threw in money for upgrades. Turns out they were really ready to sell and move on to other projects. Suddenly, I was building a new house.

The day I moved in the front yard was full of dragon-flies flitting everywhere. A sign of transformation.

Then I started meeting the neighbors... Some strange alchemy brought together a large number of people who actually want to know each other, to even hang out with each other. To craft and cook and run and fantasy football and play poker and hang out in the new pool together. That's right, last July a new amenity center opened, and it turned out the HOA likes throwing a good party just as much as the residents like going to them. Monthly cocktail hours and local bands, food trucks, parades, adult Easter egg hunts, and watching reality TV together. It's like I'm back in college and the dorms got a lot nicer.

Now, the holidays approach and I've been invited to a Halloween Party – costumes required to get in the door. My 1920's flapper costume arrived from Amazon today. I haven't dressed up since my 20's, which was a very long time ago, but I'm going all out this year! Balance is slowly returning to my life after working 24/7 nonstop for a few years. It's what I wished for last year and it showed up all year long. Strange what happens when you just put it out there in the universe. More adventures to follow.

Thank you for reading our stories! Without readers, we would be talking to…probably ourselves!

You know, I have to admire people who are willing to dress up (Halloween) or just do outrageous stuff.

I have an issue with putting myself out there having to do with my (already related) issue with feeling judged. Or put another way, rejected.

Someone hates my outfit? *Rejected*. Someone hates my joke? *Rejected*. Someone hates my Coke? Well, I guess I would reject their choice in soda. (Finally, something I have a bit of backbone about.)

There are a lot of things to be thankful for in my life, not the least is being able to tell stories and make a living doing it. I travel the world going to book fairs to learn more, meet people (who probably are a two-hour flight from my home in the USA if I could have met them there instead of here in Frankfurt, Germany), and learn more about this incredibly interesting industry.

In my own way, I get to help people who are hurting.

Some of our readers need to be taken away from their situation. Perhaps they are recovering from sickness in their home, and if they see one more episode of *Housewives* of <insert a location near you> or Kardashians, or even a show on the Food Network, they will wish for the end themselves.

Instead, they drop into our stories, and the next thing they know, it's hours later, and pain and suffering were held in abeyance.

I was reminded of the power of stories on my flight over to Germany. We had to take three flights. The first from Las Vegas to Dallas (very cramped). I read the end of *Rogue* (new story coming out in about a month or two) on the way to Dallas. Except for some adjustment because of my size in the cramped chair, the flight went FAST.

Then, after a bit of wait, we got on an American flight to London (LHR). There, I napped some (trying to handle the jetlag issues), read *Cryptid Assassin*, and tried to edit more of my *OPUS X* project (book 03).

What I noticed was even with the lack of energy due to travel sucking it out of me, the reading was cathartic and peaceful.

Even if the action was intense and harsh.

Once past LHR on the flight to Frankfurt, I did something I normally don't do... I watched a movie. I decided to watch *The Hitman's Bodyguard* with Ryan Reynolds and Samuel L Jackson. It was a fun, action-packed movie and whoever decided to pair up these two actors, I have to say GOOD CHOICE!

I finished the movie early in my morning here a day later and really like how they turned the hitman's story around to possibly being the good guy… He was effectively a vigilante for pay. I rather like that type of character (someone doing the right thing, but perhaps doing it the wrong way.)

Further, watching the show, I started to understand a bit more about relationships. So, I suspect I will do more relationships in stories in the future.

Maybe if I write enough about relationships, I'll figure out how to handle my issues with rejection and enjoy a Halloween costume party.

Ad Aeternitatem,

Michael

THE WITCH NEXT DOOR

OTHER BOOKS BY JUDITH BERENS

OTHER BOOKS BY MARTHA CARR

JOIN THE ORICERAN UNIVERSE FAN GROUP ON FACEBOOK!

CONNECT WITH THE AUTHORS

Martha Carr Social

Website: http://www.marthacarr.com

Facebook: https://www.facebook.com/
groups/MarthaCarrFans/

Michael Anderle Social

Michael Anderle Social
Website:
http://www.lmbpn.com

Email List:
http://lmbpn.com/email/

Facebook Here: https://www.
facebook.com/TheKurtherianGambitBooks/